"An academic shocker with quite a hook; one reads it in a state of frozen uneasiness. This is a contemporary chiller of and for our time, or just beyond—the achievement tests of 1984?"—*Kirkus*

"A low-key horror story that satirizes present-day big-university education. This chilling story builds to a strong climax."—*Publishers' Weekly*

Modern University—a world of multiple choice and no choice, of complete individual freedom and imposing authority. It is a world entered into willingly but from which there is no transfer.

With the keenness and force of the honed ax that figures so prominently in his story, Stephen Walton leads us into a realm where reality and nightmare converge.

"WELCOME TO MODERN UNIVERSITY"
. . . and remember—you have been warned.

NO TRANSFER

STEPHEN WALTON

CHARTER
NEW YORK

A DIVISION OF CHARTER COMMUNICATIONS INC.
A GROSSET & DUNLAP COMPANY

NO TRANSFER

Published by arrangement with The Vanguard
Press, Inc.

Charter Books
A Division of Charter Communications Inc.
A Grosset & Dunlap Company
360 Park Avenue South
New York, New York 10010

Manufactured in the United States of America

FOR MY PARENTS

PART ONE

1

I suppose I should be presenting right now some mellow sort of prologue, but I won't. Because it might not fit, and because I probably couldn't write it anyhow. I'll pick the story up where it started for me, if not for its principal, and then go back to the beginning. The point I always start from in memory was in the middle of the October of my green-tag year, when I was sitting in the suite I had then, talking with a freshman I'd just met.

There'd been a phone number on the manuscript that had landed on my desk just before time to close up. I'd picked it up, just glancing at the note from Patty that said it looked good to her, and put it into the file-folder along with the rest of the stuff I was taking home with me that evening.

I locked up the office—Patty'd already left—and took my movable paraphernalia up to the suite. After I'd listened to the news and eaten my TV dinner, I read the thing. Its title was "Life in the Tower Is as Good as Anywhere Else," and it was concerned with the satirical adventures at MU of a young man with an unspecified incurable disease. I read it again and mentally filed it to be run soon or held for the frosh issue if absolutely necessary.

After finishing up the rest of the day's paperwork and looking briefly at some essential study-material, I decided to call the author of "Life in the Tower." If his number hadn't been on the script, I probably would have been too lazy to look it up.

"Gary Fort?"

"Yes."

"Gary, this is Duncan Chase from the *Tumbrel*. I've read the story you submitted and I'd like to talk to you about it, if you don't mind."

"Sure."

"Could you come up sometime this evening?"

"I guess so."

"Fine. The number's twenty-one hundred. Just come on over. I expect to be in all evening."

"Okay. I can be over in about half an hour, if that's all right."

"Fine. At your convenience."

"Thank you."

"It's nothing. So long for now."

"So long."

I grabbed whatever it was I was reading then, put some upbeat on the phonograph, and sat down with my cigarettes near at hand.

I wasn't keeping track of the time but it was probably half an hour to the minute when I heard the knock on the door. I got up and opened it, and was faced by a very clean-looking freshman, in uniform.

"I'm Gary Fort," he said.

"Of course. Come in."

He had apparently been expecting a rather formal editorial conference. His uniform was exactly right: gray flannel trousers, white shirt, black-and-silver striped tie, black blazer with white shoulder tags perfectly aligned (so many freshmen get them on wrong). I felt guilty for my old chinos and sweater.

He took the chair I indicated to him.

"I guess I should have warned you that the *Tumbrel*'s a pretty sloppy outfit. Care for a beer?"

"Well, if it wouldn't be any trouble. . . ."

"None at all." I kept talking as I went to the kitchen. "I'd like to use that story of yours, Gary. Either run it fairly soon—it's short enough to fit in easily—or else maybe save it for the all-frosh issue."

"Thank you."

"No, thank *you* for submitting it." I opened two cans, got glasses out of the cupboard as an afterthought. "Exactly how it's going to work out remains to be seen, I'm afraid." I returned to the living room, set a glass and can down beside Gary, held on to my own. "But there's no doubt that the thing is usable, and not just as freshman material."

"Well, whatever way you want it."

"Good. Let me think." I paused and thought. "Yeah. We can put it in the first issue of next term, instead of letting it sit until this spring. You see, it's no skin off my nose if we wind up short on stuff for the frosh issue—we'll get a freshman editor to worry about that."

He nodded and paused for a few seconds. "Do I have to sign some sort of permission release?"

"Yes, but we can take care of that at the office—see Patty, at your convenience."

"Okay."

"No, what I really asked you here for was to talk about the story itself, if you don't mind."

"No, of course not."

"Okay. Now, if I see it right, you're playing on the incongruity of a guy going here who's got an incurable disease, and how safe he feels compared to everyone else. Right?"

"That, and it's a sort of parody on fatalism."

"Is there a real Cecilia somewhere?"

"Yes and no. There was a girl back home and then there's the girl I've been seeing here."

"They both like Cecilia?"

"The one back home is, a little bit. The other one isn't really at all. This Cecilia is a character I've been using in a lot of things."

"And now 'Cecilia Goes to MU.'"

"Yeah—I couldn't just leave her behind, after all."

"Of course not. . . . How did you hit on the particular tone you're using? Most people don't sound that bitter until they're sophomores at least."

"Well, I've been having some troubles lately."

Rather than say anything, I sipped at my beer.

"It's the girl I've been seeing, the one up here. I wish to hell this Paramours' Day weren't coming up so soon."

I chuckled. "No one knows for sure, but everyone says it was the ladies who pinned it down to a day every term."

"Wouldn't be surprised."

"To get back to what I was saying, you show . . . considerable advancement in disillusion. And we haven't even had a Self-Discipline Lesson yet this year." And then I went on to ask him, as I'm afraid I asked too many freshmen, what his first impressions of Modern University were like.

2

Now I'll start over again, from the beginning this time. I began to get the early part of the story that same night, from what Gary told me himself. Later on I got more of it, from Liebman, Frazier, and even Joyce. I realize I may be guilty of having made up certain details to piece the story together, but I'm sure my reconstruction is complete in essence, at least. This is the way it was:

Since he was going up a day early, he was able to get two seats to himself in the bus for this last leg of the trip. Stretching out with the seat backs down as far as they would go, he tried to make himself sleep, to catch up from the night before, when he'd done his packing at the last minute. It didn't work; the bus was getting too close to Modern.

He had seen photographs of the place but had not yet been there himself. He still wondered if he were perhaps taking a pig in a poke to come here—everything he knew about the school came from the catalogue and other printed matter, the interview he'd had, or the reputation the school had by now built up. He was willing to see for himself from here out.

These fields and woods on either side of the road, this territory was new, even if it was only fields and woods, and he expected at any moment to see the Tower come looming out up ahead.

Finally it did appear: glass, stainless steel, and concrete, without ornamentation. He didn't know exactly how tall it was, although he supposed he should. Fifty floors at least. It was startling—not the size, but that it should come rising out of an otherwise unfeatured woodscape like this. Yes, *very* Modern.

With his elbow on the window ledge, his chin in his hand pressed against the glass, he watched the building grow. Its bearing from the bus changed with variation in the direction of the road, but finally it was bracketed in. As the bus crested a hill, the small valley up ahead was opened to view, with the town of Modern, the campus of woods, fields, smaller buildings, and the Tower itself, now entirely visible.

The bus turned to spiral on down, going from the rim of the little valley toward the tower at the bottom, which he could see clearly now through his window, directly out to the side. It was enormous—big around as well as tall. He wondered how it would stack up against the competition of Manhattan.

The bus went down a street of the town, lined with trees and houses—faculty, he remembered. A gas station, a few stores, a bank, a church or two; there wasn't much to it. Then they were on the campus proper, down a broad boulevard, with the Tower up ahead, by now swelled nearly to fill the bus's front windows.

The bus turned off the boulevard onto the loop that ran up to the entrance of the Tower. Now it drove slowly alongside the face of the building. He could see panels on the first floor, of many sizes, some frosted, the rest tinted or curtained against the afternoon sun. The bus whined and slowed, pulled up by the concrete canopy projecting over the front entrance. "Modern University," the driver said, and opened the door.

He stirred in his seat—it seemed the first time in years—stretched, and stood up to get his lighter bags from the overhead rack, bending backward frequently into the area of his two seats to let other passengers by. He had no objection to being one of the last ones off. Finally he stepped out of the air-conditioned bus into the heat and onto the cement apron before the doors of the Tower.

He waited his turn to pick up his suitcase, took it with his smaller bag and his satchel in through the front doors. Then he paused to look around.

To his left, a bank of elevators. Ahead, something like an arcade, off from its sides carpeted areas of chairs and standing ashtrays, shops, a newsstand, a snack bar, and a restaurant. Halls branching off. In the middle of the arcade two wide escalators leading up to the second floor and back. To his right, a directory board, a map of the first floor, and an information desk with a girl behind it.

He stepped over to the desk and set down his bags.

"May I help you?"

"Yes, I'd like to check in."

"Freshman?"

"Uh-huh."

"Freshman check-in is on the seventeenth floor, at the desk by the elevators. We're supposed to have a sign down here, but you're a little early."

"Yes. Thank you."

He picked up his bags and went across to one of the elevators marked "Floors 1 to 20." He touched the heat-sensitive button for floor seventeen. In a second or two the door closed and he felt the thrust on his feet.

Across the hall from the elevators on the seventeenth floor was a young man seated behind a card table, a stack of stuffed Manila envelopes to his left and a bin of linen rolls to his right. On the table were a phone plugged into a wall jack, a sheaf of computer-printed papers, and what looked like a tackle box.

"I'd like to check in."

"Name?"

"Gary Fort."

"Fort . . ." The desk clerk riffled through the sheets before him, made a checkmark on one of them. "Room eighteen-fourteen." He opened the tackle box and sorted through scores of tagged keys. "Here you go. Leave your stuff there and come on back for your linen and folder."

"Thanks."

There was no card table on the eighteenth floor. A sign pointed down the hallway to the left, "To Rooms." At a T-junction of halls just beyond the elevator bank were two others. "Odd Numbers" pointing to the left, "Even Numbers" to the right.

He turned to the right, walked a short distance down the cream-colored, carpeted hall. It was flanked on both sides by walnut-colored doors with black-and-silver number plates and mail slots. He set his bags down, got out his key, and learned how to work the lock.

Little light spilled in through the open door, and most of the room was in darkness. He fumbled at the wall to the left of the door frame and found a light switch.

In the light he saw two dark blue folding partitions at either end of the left wall of the room, with a walnut desk between them, a matching straight chair pushed into its kneehole. Up against the right wall was a blue-covered sofa, which he supposed would make into a bed somehow. On the wall above the sofa were built-in bookshelves, again walnut-colored. The far wall was blank, only slightly relieved by the walnut lowboy against it. The walls were bone white, the ceiling was of white acoustical tile, the floor was fully carpeted in dark blue.

Leaving his bags by the sofa, he went to see what was on the other side of the farther partition, and found that it screened a good-sized closet. Behind the other partition was a bathroom. On one side a shower stall, and next to it a toilet with a Pullmanish pull-down sink above. The small mirror over the sink was complemented by a full-length one on the opposite wall of the bathroom, on which were also a small medicine cabinet and a towel rack.

Tentatively satisfied, he locked the room behind him and went back to the seventeenth floor. The desk clerk had to ask his name again, then made another checkmark and gave him a Manila folder and a roll of linen.

"Is there anything else?" Gary asked.

"Nope. That's it. Just take a look at the folder."

"Okay, thanks."

"That's okay. Oh, by the way, welcome to Modern University."

"Thanks." He took the folder and linen back up to the room. He decided that the only thing he really didn't like about his room was that it had no windows. He started unpacking his bags.

I was in the Tower a day early myself. In fact, I'd already been there a couple of weeks, putting an issue into shape. But that was done, and I wasn't expecting any phone calls that afternoon.

"Hello, Duncan."

"Nancy. How are you?"

"Okay. You?"

"As usual. You're back early."

"Of course."

"How was your summer?"

"Nothing to cheer about."

I nodded, then realized it wouldn't go over the phone. "I could say as much for mine . . . . You just get in?"

"Just finished unpacking."

"Could I suggest dinner?"

"If you'd like."

"Six o'clock? Tower Room?"

"Fine. I'm in twenty-twenty this year."

"Be there at six."

"See you then."

"So long." I put the receiver down and tried to go back to what I'd been reading.

Unpacking finished, Gary was reclining on his sofa, looking through the materials from his folder. All the expected things: rules, procedures, facilities, services, athletic and cultural schedules, phone books, handouts from various organizations. And, beside all these things, a copy of the *Tumbrel*, apparently a combination literary-humor magazine.

The *Tumbrel*, published at Modern University by the Student Publications Committee. Thirty-five cents a copy, first issue in autumn complimentary to freshmen. A variety of stories, poems, and articles, some apparently "serious," some not so much so, like "Campus Politics: Who, How, What, Where, When, and Why the Hell?"

Finally he packed everything back into the folder except the list of eating-places, which he consulted briefly and then pocketed. Just as he opened the door to go out, he was hit by a blast of Tchaikovsky. It was as if it had been turned on at the same instant, but then he realized that the rooms were effectively soundproofed. The music was coming through the open door of the room across the hall. Gary stuck his head inside. *"Eighteen-Twelve Overture,* isn't it?"

"Yeah." The young man inside was unpacking a suitcase. A phonograph was going on his desk. "As soon as I saw what my room number was, I knew I'd have to unpack my records first." He put out his right hand. "Keith Frazier."

Gary shook the hand. "Gary Fort. You just get in?"

"Yeah. You too?"

"Just got my stuff put away. Care to join me for dinner? I was just heading downstairs."

"Yeah, why not." Frazier shut off his phonograph and locked his room, and they took the elevator to the second floor. They wandered around in search of the cafeteria Gary's list said should be somewhere on this floor, looking into the store windows they passed. They paused before a haberdasher's, where there was displayed a black blazer on a headless half-trunk. It was shown with a white shirt and a black-and-silver striped tie. There were two small, light blue strips, one on each shoulder, like rank insignia on an old cavalry uniform.

"What's that?" Frazier said.

"I don't know."

"Is there anything about it in the folders?"

"I don't know. I haven't read that much of mine. It does look good, though."

"True. Come on, let's find that damn cafeteria."

It turned out to be a huge place at one of the back corners of the second floor. They got a table near one of the windows, and were reasonably well satisfied with what they had gotten for what they had paid. They ate rapidly, looking up only when an occasional pretty girl passed by; the place was less than half filled.

"That's really a tick-off," Gary was saying. "No windows."

"Buck up," said Frazier. "You've got more room for pictures than I do."

"Great." Gary sipped at his coffee.

"Cigarette?" Frazier held out a pack of Camels.

"No thanks, I don't smoke."

Frazier shrugged, lit up with a very old-looking lighter. "What-all are we supposed to be doing tomorrow?"

"Orientation or something. I don't know."

"Say anything about it in the folder?"

"I don't know. I'll read it tomorrow morning."

"That's the way." Frazier laughed, exhaling smoke in short bursts.

"Have you looked at the *Tumbrel* yet?"

"No."

"Some interesting-looking stuff. I suppose it's even more interesting when you know what's going on here."

At the Tower Room, we'd had no cocktails and we'd taken no wine with the meal, but now we had brandy with our coffee.

"I've always thought this room's a cheat," Nancy was saying.

I looked at her quizzically, to indicate that I wanted her to go on.

"Really. The top floor of the Tower, lots of windows, lights low inside. But there's nothing to see outside, nothing at all."

"The shining lamps of the friendly little town of Modern," I said.

"Too few and too far down."

"The moon and stars."

"You shouldn't need a place like this to see them."

I nodded. "My only excuse is that I like the food here."

She smiled. "It's good. . . . So you've been working hard?"

I nodded again. "Busy as the proverbial goddam bee. I hope no one figures out how much of the new issue I had to write myself."

"I won't tell."

I smiled. "And the timing. I still can't believe we got it out in time for the folders."

"It's a good issue, though."

"Thanks. We try. . . . I'm sorry you didn't have a better summer."

"Well, I shouldn't really complain. I was well-fed, I got enough sleep, and I had work to keep me busy."

"Don't say it so exhaustedly."

"Sorry, that's the way it is." She put out her cigarette.

"Do you want another brandy?"

"No, really, thanks."

"Do you want to go then?"

"Yes, if you don't mind."

"No." I figured out the tip and picked up the rest of my change from the little tray.

"Was dinner all right?" I asked when we were in the hallway outside the restaurant.

"Just fine. Didn't you enjoy it?"

"Yes, of course. It's just that you were so quiet most of the time."

"Can't help it." She put her arm through mine.

"I know." We took the elevators, then walked to her door. "Don't worry. I'm not expecting to be asked in."

"You understand." She unlocked the door, then pecked my lips and went inside.

Gary was playing gin with Frazier in Frazier's room, with the door open and the phonograph playing the overture again, despite Gary's protests.

"Say, that's not bad." Someone new had appeared at the door.

"I just couldn't help myself. Keith Frazier." He stood up to shake hands with the newcomer.

"Art Liebman."

"Gary Fort." Gary also got up to shake.

"I'm in eighteen-eight," said Liebman. "There's no theme for that, I'm afraid. You guys been here long?"

"Long enough to get moved in and have supper," said Frazier.

"Uh-huh. I just got in a little while ago myself."

"Did you get a window, Art?" Gary asked.

"Yeah, eighteen-eight's on this side."

Gary stuck out his tongue good-naturedly. "How come everybody lucks out but me?"

"Somebody up there loves me," said Frazier.

"Sure," Gary said.

"Actually," said Liebman, "the housing office is down on the sixth floor. And the windows are given out by lot except for the Floor Supervisors, but their rooms are bigger anyway."

"Oh," said Gary.

"Hey," said Frazier, "where's our Supervisor? I haven't seen any sign of him."

"He's probably around," Liebman said. "They don't do much. They're just here."

Gary and Frazier grunted acknowledgement. Then Gary grinned.

"That's game," said Frazier. "Try another?"

"No thanks. I'm going to try to turn in early." He stood up and stretched. "See you guys tomorrow."

22

"See you," said Frazier and Liebman.

Gary went to his room, closed the door, and made up his bed. He considered going out to explore more of the building but went to bed instead.

3

Gary woke around ten the next morning. He lay curled up, clutching his pillow as his alarm clock snarled at him. He'd put it on his desk so that he'd have to get up to shut it off. Now he growled back at it, got up, and pounced on it. Then he stood in his pajamas, scratching his head.

Groggily, he got himself showered, shaved, and dressed. After checking his folder to make sure he was free for the time being, he went downstairs. The halls along the way were crowded with his fellow students moving in. Breakfast was at the first-floor snack bar he'd seen on entering. Orange juice, toast with a plastic-packed serving of Kraft jam, coffee, and the waitress was good-looking. Two stools down there was a young man in black blazer and striped tie, like the outfit in the store window. This time the things on the shoulders were red.

Back at the room there was a note in his mailbox saying that his trunk and two packages had come for him. He called the number indicated and was told that they'd be right up. Within a few minutes they were delivered by a young man in silver-gray workclothes, and then Gary started unloading his radio, typewriter, miscellaneous junk, and the two cartons of books.

When he was almost finished, close to noon, Frazier

came over. He'd just gotten up and was about to go for breakfast. Gary agreed to come along for a second cup of coffee.

"Let me go back to the room a minute," Frazier said. "Get some stuff so I won't have to come back before those tests."

"Good idea. What are we going to need?"

"Pens and pencils, I guess. Admission Certificate for sure, probably ought to take the brochure along too."

"Okay."

They went to the snack bar. Gary studied his orientation brochure while he sipped his coffee.

"Yeah," Frazier said between bites of toast. "Where are we supposed to go?"

"Ummmm. . . . Student numbers ending in zero through three report to room nine-A for testing; four to six to room nine-B; seven to nine to room nine-C."

"We're numbers now?"

"Yeah, sure. Look at your Admission Certificate."

Frazier pawed through his pockets, brought out the card. "Five-seven-nine-eight-four."

Gary had his out too. "Mine's five-seven-two-three-oh."

"Congratulations."

When the time came, Gary was to go to room nine-A, Frazier to nine-B. They parted at the ninth-floor lobby.

"Best of luck," said Frazier. "Give 'em hell."

"Right. And if I'm not out in two hours, attack."

Room nine-A was set up to double as lecture room and auditorium. Close to four hundred young men and women were filling in its seats.

"Hey, Gary!" Liebman called from down near the front.

"Hi, Art." Gary took the seat next to him. "All set?"

"Why not? You?"

"Guess so. Any idea what these tests are like?"

26

"Sort of like the SAT's. Nothing to get nervous about."

Gary nodded, got out his pens and pencils.

Then at twelve forty-five a man in shirt sleeves called for order. A roll was read of those who were supposed to be present; question booklets, answer sheets, and machine-scoring pencils were passed out, and the actual testing began.

No one was dismissed until all the papers were collected. Gary finished early, checked and rechecked his answers, and still had time left to get thorough looks at the girls who were assisting the test administrator.

When they were let out there was a great crush to the doors. Gary and Liebman managed to find Frazier in the lobby, sitting down with a cigarette.

"My group got out a little early," he said. "How'd you like it?"

Liebman grunted and Gary spread his hands.

"Yeah," Frazier said. "At least that's it until the Convocation."

The three went down to the shopping floors to browse and catch a late lunch. Then it was up to room four-E for the Freshman Convocation. The room turned out to be a medium-sized auditorium. They got seats midway between front and back, and watched as their classmates came in to fill the room.

A young man came out and adjusted the microphone on the rostrum. He wore the black blazer, the tie that seemed always to go with it, and a gray shirt. The tabs on his shoulders were light blue, like the ones in the store window. He blew into the mike and the bursts of rushing air came clearly over the loudspeakers. "Can you hear me all right?"

There was a general murmur of assent.

"Okay, then. I'm Tom Curtis, president of Student Government for this year, and your host for this afternoon. We've got a brief but, we think, relevant program for you today. This is, after all, our one big chance to welcome you into the warm fold of Modern University."

Small spots of laughter in the audience.

"Well, I can see we've got you with us right from the start."

More laughter, more open now.

"Anyway, we hope you'll at least have the courtesy to stay with us for the rest of the program. Appearing with me this afternoon will be Mr. Ernest Barnett, Director of Admissions—" Barnett, in a dark gray suit, walked onto the stage and took a seat; "Duncan Chase, editor of the *Tumbrel*—" very properly in uniform, I left the wings and took my seat; "—and Dr. John Clark, President of the University, will be coming in a little later.

"First off, let me formally and officially welcome you to Modern University. I think you know by now that our school is unique. Speaking as a senior, let me tell you that you should find your years here among the most fruitful—and enjoyable—of your lives. Our academic programs and facilities are surpassed by none in the country. So much for chauvinism—but it *is* true. Our social facilities are unparalleled too. As Mr. Barnett and Dr. Clark will probably tell you again, MU is a community of adults. This may be something of a change for you. But I think you'll appreciate this treatment and find that it's really more fun."

Scattered titters.

"All right, you don't know that I meant it *that* way. Wait and see. Remember that while it's very easy to have a good time here, it's not all gravy. Anyhow, that about sums up my remarks, apart from a pitch for Student Government, and I'll try to make that short. You're all poten-

28

tial leaders or you wouldn't be here. Some of you will have just a little more talent or inclination in that line than your fellows. We want you. As time goes on, you'll learn just how much Student Government actually does here. Our responsibility is ten times that of analogous organizations at other schools, ten times or more. Consequently, our demand for talent is at least ten times as great. Some of you—many of you, I hope—will want to take part with us. Believe me, we're ready to welcome you. That's about it for the sales pitch.

"And now, let me introduce the man who's passed judgment on all of us, our Director of Admissions, Mr. Ernest Barnett."

Applause as Curtis sat down and Barnett took the rostrum.

"Good afternoon, ladies and gentlemen, and again, welcome to Modern University. There are one thousand and twelve of you. You represent fifty states and twenty-two foreign countries. All of you graduated within the top ten per cent of your high school or preparatory school class. Over a hundred of you are Merit Scholars. Seventy per cent of you are receiving financial aid from one source or another. You are, in other words, a very good group.

"And you know what Modern University offers. What it promises, and what it threatens. You knew when you chose to come here. You should be able to make it. We've selected you carefully enough so that if you don't, it will be your own fault. That's about all I've got to say. Thank you. Tom?"

"Thank you, Mr. Barnett." During polite applause, Curtis took the mike again. "And now Duncan Chase has a few words. Duncan?"

I stood up and Curtis sat down. The audience was wondering if it should be applauding again; a few were trying.

29

"Thanks, Tom." I adjusted the mike and my tie. "Well, I hope you aren't expecting that I'll be providing comic relief. All I've got for you, I'm afraid, is another pitch. As Tom said, I edit the *Tumbrel* and that's why I'm here. If you've looked at your copy—it's in your folder, along with everything else—if you've looked at your copy, you know that the *Tumbrel* is MU's 'literary' and humor magazine. The reason for the name, if it's not immediately obvious to you, will be clear soon enough. So I'm making a pitch for the *Tumbrel*. I think it's important. I'm asking you for submissions—I know a lot of you would be making them even without the request, but I'm making it anyway. I'm also asking you for your support—asking you to buy the magazine and to read it. I'll be making these same requests again, in every issue, on posters and over the Radio Service, just as I'm making them now.

"I've said that I think the *Tumbrel* is important. My opinion is that it is MU looking at itself, free to like or dislike what it sees. In many ways, I feel, the *Tumbrel* is the conscience of Modern University. If the need for a conscience isn't evident to you, I ask that you wait a little while, or take one of the many ethics courses offered.

"So that's about it for me. My apologies for not having any good jokes ready. But despite the apparent tone of the magazine—no, its *genuine* tone—I'm serious about the *Tumbrel*. It's one of the most serious things going on around here. Thank you."

More of the polite applause as I surrendered the mike to Curtis.

"Thanks, Duncan. And now," Curtis said, "it's my pleasure to introduce the man who runs it all, the President of Modern University, Dr. John Clark." Curtis turned to face the wings and began clapping. The rest of us on the stage stood up to applaud, and the audience joined in. Dr. Clark came out and stepped up to the rostrum.

"Thank you, Tom." He cleared his throat and adjusted the mike while the applause gradually faded out and we at the back of the stage sat down again.

"Good afternoon, ladies and gentlemen, and welcome. That was probably the last time most of you will ever applaud me. The reason is that, among other things, I am responsible for the Self-Discipline Plan. You all know what it is, so I needn't explain it except to reiterate that it's the soul of Modern University. The opening of the University and the initiation of the Plan were simultaneous. When the Self-Discipline Plan ends, so does Modern University. The one is that important to the other.

"Your folders and the gentlemen here on the stage with me have told you just about everything you need to know to start your careers here. All that is left for me is to give you a warning.

"Some of you, when first told about the Self-Discipline Plan during your interviews, may not have believed what you were told. Some of you may still think that we are not serious about this. We *are*. This is the other side of the coin of adult treatment. We want you to be serious students, and you know you'd better be. There are one thousand twelve of you here today. More than a thousand of you will graduate from Modern University, thoroughly prepared for further studies or to start work. You will not be allowed, as you know, to transfer to other institutions, and there is no disciplinary expulsion here, so your numbers will not be diminished in those ways. But a few of you, a very few but still a definite number, will provide Self-Discipline Lessons for your fellow students. Others of you will bear the ultimate responsibility for presenting such Lessons. No one can say at this time who will fall into what group. But some of you will be examples, and some of you will help to make these examples graphic. Do you understand?

"I hope that at least some of you have learned by now that nothing is free in this world. You are provided here with the best faculty and facilities possible. You are bound only by the minimum rules necessary to maintain simple order. You are placed in an environment that may seem to some of you more like a country club, or perhaps even a red-light district, than a university. You are treated as adults. The price is responsibility, the responsibility of adults, which implies a certain risk. But you should not be gambling with yourselves.

"We believe that Modern University, *with* its Self-Discipline Plan, provides the training and background best suited to survival in our flawed modern world—and to success in it, if you want it. The records of our graduates are continuously bearing us out.

"Some of you may think that we are simply giving you 'enough rope.' This is not so. We want each one of you to succeed here—we want this very much. Unfortunately, statistics show us that a certain number of you will not succeed here. If I could know who among you these are, I would ask them now to leave. But I don't know, I can't know, before you have begun. I know that each of you *can* succeed here—Mr. Barnett has seen to that. But I also know that not all of you will. This is why I offer you a warning now. I offer it to you sincerely and, in all seriousness, I ask that you take it and consider it very carefully. Thank you."

Applause started and grew. Curtis, Barnett, and I came to our feet, clapping. Clark smiled now, for the first time, then walked off into the wings.

Curtis took the mike again. "That's it for today, ladies

32

and gentlemen. Thank you very much, and we'll see you all at registration. Good afternoon."

There was a last scattering of applause and then the frosh were moving out.

Gary, Liebman, and Frazier had supper that night in the cafeteria on the second floor—decent, modest meals, with prices to match. The place was nearly full tonight. Great numbers of the black blazers, on which the tags might be red, green, or blue.

"Do you want to go to the mixer?" Gary asked over the coffee while the other two were busy lighting cigarettes.

"Sounds like fun." Liebman waved out a match.

"Yeah, sure," said Frazier. "Where is it?"

Gary dug his orientation brochure out of a pocket. "Roof, weather permitting."

"Okay," said Frazier. "What's the weather like? I haven't been outdoors today."

"Try looking out the window," Gary said.

The weather visible through the nearest window was fine. There were no clouds to be seen, and the sun was hanging red on the rim of the valley.

"Okay, looks like it'll be on the roof." Frazier took a luxuriant puff on his cigarette. "What time does it start?"

"Eight-thirty." Gary took a sip of his coffee. "There's no rush."

Frazier nodded.

Liebman set his coffee cup down. "The upperclassmen will be in charge anyhow."

"Oh, I don't know," Frazier said. "What have they got that we haven't got?"

"Black blazers, for one thing."

"Okay, Art," Gary said, "can you explain them?"

33

"I can try. They're uniforms of a sort. The color of the shoulder tags indicates class. Blue for seniors, green for juniors, red for sophomores, white for freshmen."

"Does everybody wear them?" Frazier asked.

"Not everybody. They're not required, of course."

"Of course," said Frazier.

"Yeah," said Gary, "but they do look good. By the way, Art, can I ask how you know about all these things?"

"Oh, I had a cousin graduate from here last year. See, now you know the secret of my omniscience. Anyhow, the uniforms are just part of the rush on the freshman girls."

"How's that?" Gary said.

"It's a little thing the upperclassmen have got going for themselves," Liebman said. "They've got the uniforms, they've got the bigger rooms or suites, and they've got the parties going."

"Sounds like a good deal," said Gary.

"Sure," said Frazier, "all we have to do is wait a year."

Gary smiled. "You mean you want to skip the mixer?"

"Hell, no. I'm not going to be scared off that easily."

"You're going, aren't you, Art?"

"Sure."

"Okay," Gary said. "So we'll give 'em hell, even if we are freshmen."

After a while they drifted back to the rooms to make their preparations. The brochure indicated coat and tie for the mixer, so Gary put on a reliable combination of black knit tie and gray tweed jacket, then picked out a book to read until eight-thirty.

The roof was open to the sky, but its edge was well fenced in and plastic panels had been set up to keep most of the wind off, which otherwise would have been stiff this far up. There was even a temporary dance floor down. A band was set up by the stairwell entrance near the middle. A baritone saxophone, drums, two electric guitars, and an electric bass, thumping it out.

Gary, Frazier, and Liebman took stock as well as they could. Maybe five couples were dancing. A few people, singles apparently, were sitting at tables set up around the outside. The refreshment stand in a corner was doing a very modest business. It was 8:45.

"Great turnout," said Frazier.

"These things always start slowly," Liebman said.

"Shall we grab a table?" Gary asked.

"Let's grab some refreshments first," Frazier said.

The others immediately nodded in agreement.

"Three drafts," Frazier said to the young man behind the counter of the stand.

Gary and Liebman began digging for change—twenty cents a glass for Budweiser up here.

"That's okay. I'll cover this round." This met with no complaints. Each got a good-sized glass, and Frazier indicated a table.

From there they got good looks at everyone coming up the stairs. They sat quietly, sipping their beers. Frazier and Liebman had cigarettes. Every so often one of the three would point out for comment some particular girl coming up the stairs.

"Shall I go get another round?" Gary asked.

"Yeah," said Frazier.

"Hey," Liebman said, "there's that guy who talked today. What's-his-name, Chase."

"He's not wearing his uniform," Gary said.

"He wouldn't have to," Frazier said. "Now would he?"

Gary grunted and went off to get the next round. When

all were about halfway through it, Liebman announced that he was going to try his luck. There was something of a genuine crowd by now, mostly standing and watching the few couples dancing.

Watching Liebman work his way into the mob, and listening to the competent rock being played and sung, Gary was beginning to think even he might give it a try sooner or later.

"What the hell." Frazier got up and moved into the crowd.

Gary was left sitting with the three glasses and an ashtray full of cigarette butts. Finally he took a last sip from his glass and got up.

As predicted, there were a great many of the black blazers in the crowd, and these seemed more often to be dancing than standing. Gary spotted a good-looking girl at the edge of the pack and moved toward her, planning to ask her to dance as soon as the present song ended. He didn't move fast enough, and she danced with a red-tag sophomore.

Gary moved on. He noticed that Liebman was dancing with a decent-looking one, and Frazier was grinding it out with a real stunner.

Gary picked out another girl, moved in from behind, and had her out on the dance floor before the competition could arrive. He found himself swinging easily with the beat, repeating the familiar lyrics subvocally. He looked at his partner and saw that she was doing a conscientious job. He smiled at her and she smiled back.

Then the tune ended and she said thank you and left. He danced a few more, each one with a different girl, including one who on a slow tune held herself so that her breasts came within a millimeter of his chest but did not touch it. On another slow number he caught the first girl he'd danced with; she came up close and acted contented.

"Say, could I buy you a beer?" he asked when the song had ended and before she could thank him for the dance.

"No, thanks." She slipped away again.

After what seemed like a decent interval of more dancing, again without results, he went back to the table. Frazier was already there.

"What happened with that girl you were with?" Gary asked him.

"Oh, we had a couple of dances and I liked the way she wiggled her pelvis, so I asked if I could buy her a beer. She said no, so I asked her if she'd like to buy me one instead. She left right after that." He drained off what was left in his glass.

"Yeah, that's about what happened to me."

Liebman returned to the table.

"What happened?" Frazier asked. "We thought maybe you had something going."

"She said she'd said she'd meet her next-door neighbor later. At least I got her name."

"That's something," Gary said.

"Yeah," said Frazier, "if it's really her name."

Liebman shrugged. "My round, isn't it?"

After watching a while longer, as the black-blazered ones cut the male frosh to tatters, they decided to move downstairs, where drafts were a nickel cheaper.

They found a quiet bar on the twelfth floor and sat at a table, a pitcher in the middle.

"Shall I say I told you so?" Liebman said.

"Okay," said Frazier, "so we just have to wait a year."

"Maybe not," Liebman said. "After all, there's a mixer every Friday night."

Gary and Frazier nodded, each making plans for the next time.

4

Gary woke with plenty of time for a leisurely breakfast before seeing his adviser. Over his coffee he went through his catalogue again, check-marking the courses that looked particularly interesting. From these he made up a tentative program, listing alternative courses in a few cases. The total came to eighteen quarter-credits, a fair load.

At nine-thirty he went to his adviser's office on the thirtieth floor. Another student was inside talking with Dr. Philip Loft. Gary waited just outside the door, juggling his catalogue, pen, and notebook as he went over his program outline once more.

The other student came out, nodding to Gary. "Come on in," Dr. Loft called.

Gary entered the office. Its shelves were crammed with heavy-looking technical books. Bound volumes and loose copies of the *Physical Review* were everywhere. Gary sat down in a chair facing the desk.

"You're . . . ?"

"Fort, Gary Fort."

"Ah, yes. Good morning, Gary. I'm Phil Loft." He put out his right hand and Gary half-rose to shake it. "Now then . . ." Loft pawed through a stack of file-folders on his desk, pulled one out, and opened it before him. "Okay, you're Gary J. Fort, entering freshman, majorless for now, graduated this past June from White Plains High School. I'll be your adviser as long as you're without a major, and afterwards as well, should you happen to decide on physics. Have you got some courses in mind?"

Gary handed him the sheet of paper with his suggested program.

"Hmmm . . . American Issues One, of course . . . Introduction to Fiction, History of Film, Calculus Three —you've had equivalents of One and Two?"

"Yes, I was given waiver of them through the Advanced Placement exams."

Loft was rummaging through the folder. "Oh yes, here it is. Fine . . . and Ancient History One. It seems like none of my majorless advisees want to take any Physics. Very sad . . . I take it you don't want a gym course. Do you think you can pass the fitness test?"

"Well, I'm not really much of an athlete, but this past summer I was swimming as often as I could and I played quite a bit of tennis."

"All right, for now at least. Just don't let the elevators do everything for you. Try to keep up some activities during the year."

Gary nodded.

"Okay. Your program looks all right, but you'll need some course alternates. You know how registration works, don't you? It's like a huge pari-mutuel operation. Everybody's course selections go into the computer, and it juggles the whole works and comes out with final schedules and class lists. The only trouble is that you don't always get exactly what you want."

Gary nodded again, and got out a second sheet of paper on which he had listed his alternate courses. Dr. Loft approved them.

"Okay, then, you're set. Here's the rest of what you'll need for registration." Loft handed Gary a small Manila envelope.

"Isn't there anything you're supposed to sign?"

Loft shook his head. "Not a thing. I'm your adviser—quite literally. You're free to make up any program you like and toss it into the hopper. All you're asked to do is come and talk to me, and the fact that you've got the rest of your registration materials is proof that you've done that. Okay?"

"Okay."

"Good enough. I'm sorry I'm so rushed today. Things are a lot easier during the term proper, believe me. Be sure to stop in any time you've got any questions or problems."

"Thank you." Gary and Dr. Loft rose simultaneously and shook hands again.

"You're welcome. See you."

Registration was running from nine-thirty to five-thirty, processing five hundred students an hour, or eight point three a minute. Ten lines ran across a large hall on the fourth floor, with detours for those with special problems.

Gary went through it calmly enough, trading quips with Frazier, whose scheduled time of entrance was the same. They followed the progress of the lines like conscientious sheep, filing their suggested programs, with alternates, paying their money, filling out information cards, having their ID pictures taken, and receiving their validated identification.

"That wasn't so bad," Gary said as they left.

"No," said Frazier. "Now all we have to do is wait and see what we get."

"When do the schedules come out?"

"They start delivering them around six, I think."

After lunch they went prowling again among the shops on the first three floors. The excuse was that they would buy their books if they could return them if they didn't get all their courses.

They passed the haberdasher's again, and Gary decided to go inside and try to find out more about the "uniform." Frazier followed.

"Of course the uniform is strictly unofficial," the young clerk was saying. "Let's see, you're about . . . Yes, this should be about right." He took one of the blazers from a rack. "This is it. All wool flannel, fully lined, two inside pockets. This is the style that's been accepted by all groups. Traditional. The buttons are lacquered sterling, with the University seal."

Gary took a close look at one of them. At the center was an image of the Tower. Circling it were the words "Modern University" and "Commitment to Excellence."

"The jacket is worn with gray trousers," the clerk went on, "with a light gray or white shirt and a black-and-silver striped tie or ascot. Class-tags on the shoulders and term ribbons over the breast pocket."

"Term ribbons?"

"For grades. A black one for high range, a gray one for middle range, and a red one for low range."

"Oh . . ." Gary said. "Uh, what's the price?"

"The blazer is forty-five dollars—they are available for less, but we think ours are worth the difference in price. The slacks are fifteen, shirts are six, tie and ascot two-fifty each. Shoulder tags are included in the price of the jacket, term ribbons are fifty cents each. Would you care to try the jacket or trousers on?"

"Well, I really don't think so today." Gary proceeded to excuse himself and was given a leaflet on "Whys and

Hows of the MU Unifor... one too.

From the haberdasher's the... Book Exchange, where they caugh... sured that they could return their pu... days for a full refund. With confidenc... clerk's help, they rounded up their texts. G... new ones—he didn't like the idea of using boo... been marked by strangers. They put their receipt... places and stopped next at a drugstore fountain to... Cokes and preview their texts. As it worked out, eac... spent more time looking at the other's than his own. On... the way out, Gary bought a *New Yorker* from the magazine rack.

"Keeping up your ties with home?" Frazier asked.

"No, I just thought I'd do what I could to help with the uplift of those from the backwoods, like you."

"Well, I'll tell you," Frazier said, with his hand to the side of his mouth, "Detroit isn't *really* the backwoods any more."

"I would never have known," Gary said. "What is, then?"

"San Francisco. Let's go."

They passed another men's store, which also displayed the uniform.

"Want to check their price?" Frazier asked.

"Sure."

The blazer was the important item—Gary already had quite suitable gray slacks. The price here was thirty.

"Well, which one are you going to buy?" Frazier asked when they were walking down the hall again.

"Neither, for now."

"That's the right attitude."

Frazier's doorway,
ing chess. Liebman
is schedule too, and

ry found that he'd
he alternate, Frazier

er said.
schedule before buy-
a mutually free hour
storm the Exchange.

on the way out. Frazier took
went to the University
a clerk and were reas-
hases within thirty
and with the
y bought all
that had
in safe
ve

"Not literally, but I do have a date. That girl I met last night, I called her this afternoon. We're going to dinner, and then to the movie."

"So she did give you her right name," Frazier said.

"Uh-huh. See you later."

"Have a good time," Gary said. Then he and Frazier finished their game. Gary lost, because of a blunder that cost him a rook.

"Another?" Frazier asked.

"No thanks. I'm going to see if I can get started with my books."

"Conscientious lad."

Gary grunted. "You've got an eight o'clock class too, don't you?"

"Yeah, I suppose I'll have to get up around seven."

"How about the first one up wake the other?"

"Okay."

"Good enough. I'd better go get to the books." Gary went to his own room and took his books out of the shopping bag on the desk. Out with them came the leaflet about the uniform, by Duncan Chase. This, naturally, was what Gary started reading first.

"The wearing of uniforms at Modern University started as a joke; it is still to be taken lightly. Almost six years ago, a campus political group, the Full Implications Party (FIP), campaigned for a block of Student Government offices with a platform of carrying, rather whimsically, certain aspects of University life to their ultimate logical ends. The platform recommended that all students walk in cadence, that reveille and taps be piped into all rooms at 5:00 A.M. and 10:00 P.M. respectively, and that, among other things, all students be required to wear uniforms. The FIP didn't expect to win the election, and it didn't win the election. But the idea of a uniform caught on.

"This idea was seen to fulfill a long-present need. MU students, perhaps paradoxically, have always tended to take pride in their University, and the wish to identify with it, for better or for worse, is strong. Something distinctive was needed, but something that would also be correct at all times, provided certain simple rules were followed. In the light of the FIP's original satiric impulse, and in the light of the desire to end sartorial doubt, the MU uniform seemed a very, very good idea.

"After a certain amount of editorial pressure from the MU *Daily Bulletin*, a study committee was appointed by Student Government. The uniform proposed by FIP obviously would not do—silver-colored khaki, with black leather Sam Brownes, student numbers on plastic badges, and knee-high black boots, for both male and female students. After lengthy deliberations, the study committee came up with the present uniform and its accepted variations, and with the NIKA plan.

"Standing for 'New Indicators of Klass Affiliation,' this turned out to be the system of red, white, blue, and green epaulettes to show class standing. The rather weak excuse given for spelling "Class" with a K was that of avoidance of any suggestion of *social* classes. Actually, it was done in

45

order to make the acronym work, and the historians on the committee had their joke.

"With the stipulation that it never be required for anything, the suggested uniform, NIKA included, was adopted by Student Government, and the adoption was quickly ratified by all groups. Soon male students were being seen more and more often wearing black blazers with NIKA tags, and ties striped with black and silver. The ladies' version of the uniform, however, never did catch on. . . ."

There was more: the rules—how to wear the uniform when, and with what possible variations; a discussion of term ribbons; mention of the significance of a tiny silver ax, to which few were entitled and which even fewer wore, on a black term ribbon.

Gary put the leaflet into a desk drawer. Setting his radio on the unobtrusive-music frequency of the University Radio Service, he finally got down to his textbooks and did spend a good amount of time with them.

5

His first day of classes followed naturally enough. Trying to set a good precedent for himself, he got up at seven. After stepping across the hall in his pajamas to wake Frazier, he took his shower and shave calmly. Not really knowing how to dress for class, he wore a jacket—his reliable gray tweed—without a tie. He was just putting the jacket on when Frazier knocked on his door.

"You about ready to go?"

"Just a minute. Come on in."

Frazier was wearing charcoal wash slacks and a solid navy sport shirt, had two spiral notebooks and two of his texts in one hand. "Well!"

"Okay, so tomorrow I'll know what to wear." Gary clipped a pen and mechanical pencil into his shirt pocket, gathered up his notebook and the books he would need for the morning.

Classes went well enough. Much of the time this first day was taken up by clerical work, very ordinary first-day-of-classes stuff, the same practically everywhere. The fringe benefit deriving from the great mechanicalness of the day was that Gary found himself with plenty of opportunity to survey his classmates. He appraised the young ladies: there were many bright-looking but also unfortunate-looking ones; but there were almost as many pretty ones. He also discovered that he was perhaps a bit overdressed; but that could and would be remedied tomorrow.

In his History of Film class there was one particular girl. It was a small class in a small room. Before and after the presence of the instructor there had been goalless conversation. He had been chatting with those on his side of the room; the particular girl, on the other side, had talked with her neighbors. It had not worked out so that he spoke to her or she to him. But tomorrow . . .

His classes for the day over by three, he found a carpeted lounge on the third floor and there made something of a dent in the mass of his reading assignments. Around five he returned to his room and straightened it up a bit.

Liebman and Frazier came by a little later and the three of them had dinner in a restaurant Frazier had discovered that afternoon. Back at the rooms, Frazier suggested a session of cards and was given two rainchecks. After that, everyone hit the books.

At ten, however, the need for a study-break was recognized by all, and they went downstairs for refreshments.

"Hey, Art," Gary said over the Cokes, "do you know anything about this Paramours' Day?" Gary had looked at some more of his folder material before getting down to studying, and had noticed the day set at October sixteenth on a calendar.

"Oh, yeah," Liebman said, "that's the MU version of Valentine's Day, only it comes once each term. That's the day when couples declare themselves paramours."

"Okay," said Gary, "what are paramours? They don't mean the term in Malory's sense, do they?"

"Just about," Liebman said. "When a couple are paramours, they're—they're a couple."

"Is this the local version of going steady?" Frazier asked.

"More or less. Since 'going steady' smacks too much of

high school, and since there's no pinning with the clubs."

"Big deal," Frazier said.

"Wait a second," Gary said. "I believe being paramours implied a bit more than going steady. Paramours were supposed to be lovers, weren't they—in the sense of mating as much as of romance?"

"Yeah," said Liebman. "If paramours are sleeping together, it's completely accepted—not that anyone talks about it."

"Sounds like good old-fashioned free love," Frazier said.

"More like free marriage," Liebman said. "It allows recognition of more or less permanent couples. Some of the parties the clubs hold, only paramours can go as couples."

"Sounds reasonable," Gary said.

"I'm told," Liebman said, "that the pairing-off around here is fantastic."

"I suppose there's some outward sign of this condition?" Frazier said.

"Oh, of course. Paramours exchange 'favours'—each wears something of the other's."

"Onward the cause of transvestism!" said Frazier.

"Come on," said Gary.

The discussion drifted away from the topics of paramours and Paramours' Day. Soon they all went back to their rooms and to their books.

The next day Gary took a different seat in History of Film. He was deliberately casual about it, loitering in the hall outside the classroom until the particular girl had gone inside, then sauntering in after a proper lapse of time and taking the seat next to hers, as if at random. After getting his notebook open to the proper section for this class, taking a pen from his pocket, he spoke to her.

"Say, what do you think of Eaton so far?" Eaton was

the name of the professor. Gary was afraid his question had come out sounding insufficiently off-the-cuff.

She didn't seem to notice, or if she had noticed, not to mind. "Oh, he seems all right, so far. It's hard to tell this early."

"True . . . I thought you might have had him for a class before."

"Me? I'm just a freshman."

"That's funny. I thought sure you were an upper."

"No, just a freshman straight out of Mamaroneck High."

"Really? I'm from White Plains."

"Do you know John Taylor?"

"No. Do you know Monica Wilson?"

"Uh-uh."

The "do you know" routine continued through a few more names without bearing fruit. Then Eaton came in and the hour got under way. He was using his class list to familiarize himself with the names of the students. This was lucky for Gary, as Eaton soon identified the girl as Miss Cleland, Joyce Cleland. Now that he knew her name, Gary could learn room and phone numbers easily enough. His own name came up soon, and that completed the introduction.

At the end of the class, with Eaton taking detailed questions up front, Gary paused before leaving. "See you Monday, Joyce."

"See you, Gary."

When he was back at his room after classes, at three that afternoon, he looked her up in the phone book and read over her number three or four times. He was strongly tempted to call her and ask for a date for tonight or tomorrow, Saturday night. He thought better of it, shut the phone book, and did some puttering about, preparatory to doing some studying.

That evening he had a rather late supper with Frazier. Liebman was not with them, already out on his date. After supper they scouted the Friday-Night Mixer, and after doing very little mixing with no results, they went to one of the quieter bars.

Getting into his room around one, Gary realized that he was probably drunk. He didn't mind. He was up on his work, for now at least, and he'd planned tomorrow as something of a holiday anyhow. He went through the routine of getting to bed in ponderous detail. He was thinking about this paramour business—seemed like a good idea. And then of Joyce. Lying with his arms around his pillow, he was soon asleep.

6

After a noonish Saturday rising and a hunched-over breakfast consisting mainly of coffee, Gary wondered what he was going to do with the rest of the day. He'd been pretty good about his studying during the week; the assignments for Monday he could complete easily enough tomorrow afternoon. No, the rest of today was to be occupied with something more or less recreational. He wished he could be seeing Joyce. But he had gotten himself fouled up often enough in the past by trying to rush things. This was college, boy. This was for record.

So he spent the day buying himself a bottle—Jack Daniels' green label; a book—*This Side of Paradise*; and a print for the blank wall of his room—a Buffet, whose work he knew and liked, of the Place de la Concorde, in grayed tones and angular, brittle lines, and totally depopulated. And that night he went to the movie with Frazier. Sunday afternoon he studied and Sunday night he started on the book and the bottle and hung his picture.

During the week he found himself getting to know Miss Joyce Cleland better and asked her to dine with him the following Saturday night. She accepted. For the first screening session he chanced taking along a bag of popcorn. Joyce was startled at first, but by no means displeased. They ate popcorn together while watching "The

Great Train Robbery" and some Méliès trickery, trying to munch quietly. The professor noticed but did not seem to mind.

Before one class Gary made a trivial joke about the Self-Discipline Plan. Joyce laughed at it, but only to be friendly, it seemed. Gary made a mental note to refrain from such jokes in the future.

Friday night Gary spent alone. Frazier had found himself a girl, was out with her, and had left his room and records in Gary's keeping. Gary played records in no order, always taking whatever was next on the stack, and learned that Frazier leaned to the early Romantics, opera, and rock and roll, with spatterings of Strauss, Bartok, show music, and, of course, Tchaikovsky.

The *Eroica* was on when Gary saw flashes of lightning outside the window. Putting Fitzgerald aside, he opened the window and discovered to his pleasure that although it was raining hard by now, it wasn't coming in on this side of the building. He turned off the lights in the room and stood at the open window as the music continued. The random thunder fitted in somehow, and the lightning showed him great stretches of grass and stands of trees, in blue-green flashes.

The symphony ended and the storm rumbled away almost simultaneously. He turned on the lights, put the next record on without looking to see what it was, and sat down again with his book. He finished it at two-thirty and Frazier came in shortly afterward.

The following afternoon, Gary set out on a hike. Liebman had said over dinner during the week that it was much easier to get a girl to go for a walk with you than to get her to come to your room. And despite obvious disadvantages, a degree of privacy could be found outdoors. Aware of his rather self-confident meticulousness, Gary

54

decided to go out that afternoon to familiarize himself with the campus and perhaps determine where a coeducational walk might end.

With his back to the Tower, he could have been made to believe that it didn't exist. Ahead, on the other side of the road, were grass, trees, bushes, all gradually sloping up a hillside that led to the rim of the valley. The breeze touched him, with only a very small, politely threatening chill in it. Coming out was a pleasurable little shock.

He learned as much as he could of the campus that afternoon. He learned paths through pines and just-browning oaks and maples; he learned the way to the power plant, the prosaic building that made possible the Tower's life; he discovered the lake beyond the trees, scattered with last-chance couples in canoes and sailboats.

At first he was sorry that he was alone on an afternoon like this, then he forgot that he was alone. He had conversations with squirrels and whistle-talks with birds. He realized that he was being very happily nutty.

Not until he was on his way to pick up Joyce at her room did Gary realize that this afternoon was the first time he'd been outdoors in almost two weeks. He decided not to go that long again, no matter what the weather.

Properly coated and tied, he arrived at her door and knocked. There was no wait. There she was, in a simple navy dress and high heels.

"Hi," said Gary.

"Hi," said Joyce.

"All set?"

"Uh-huh." She locked her room and they were off. On the way there was amiable chatter about their common class and specifically about the current assignment.

Their destination was the Tower Room, which Liebman had recommended. Gary had cased it one evening during the week and figured it would do. He and Joyce entered the restaurant and were shown to a small table not too far from a window.

"I've never really been here before, you know," Gary said after they were seated. "I hope it will be all right."

"It certainly looks nice."

Gary nodded. "I'm still amazed how many different places there are in this building."

"I know. I wonder if I'll ever get used to it."

"Oh, that shouldn't be *too* hard. It's just like a one-building high school, only on a presumably higher level."

"You don't really mean 'presumably.' You know what high standards the University has."

"But it took me, didn't it?"

Joyce smiled. "I know you're bright. You'd have to be, to think of bringing popcorn to film class."

"Well . . ." Gary brushed his fingernails on his lapel.

A waiter came with ice water and menus. He remained while Gary became confused over his menu.

"Perhaps a cocktail to start with?" the waiter suggested. He was apparently student help; perhaps he'd been in the same spot himself.

"Yes, I think so. Joyce?"

"A martini?" she said.

"Two martinis," Gary said.

The waiter nodded and went off, leaving the menus behind. Gary and Joyce kept reading.

"How about the coq au vin?" Gary finally suggested.

"Okay."

"Fine."

The waiter came back with the martinis and took their orders. Appetizer, soup, salad, vegetables—Gary was amused at repeating Joyce's distinctly spoken selections to the waiter, and still a bit confused by the ranges of choice and his own lack of knowledge.

"And to drink?"

"Joyce, did you want wine with dinner?"

"Well . . ."

"Ummm . . ." Gary was reading as rapidly as possible the wine list clipped to the menu.

"May I suggest the Chablis?" the waiter said. "We have a very good vintage."

"If you think so. Joyce?"

She nodded.

"Fine."

"The Chablis, then." The waiter took the menus and left.

Gary picked up his martini. "I really don't know anything about that sort of thing."

"That's all right." Joyce raised her own glass and sipped from it.

"Well, I'm glad he saved me." Gary sipped from his own glass and felt the first shock of a strong solution of alcohol. "But of course he couldn't just stand there and let me make a complete boor of myself."

"Of course not."

"Now, back home it's a little easier."

Although they still had not discovered any people they knew in common in Westchester, they now found that there were two or three bars there with which both were acquainted.

"Maybe we've seen each other before and don't know it," Joyce said.

"Impossible. I would have remembered you." This was tossed off lightly, the lightness lip service to anti-romanticism and the compliment sincerely meant.

57

"Oh, I'm sure I could be forgotten."

"Hardly."

They talked through their martinis and through the wine and the coq au vin with its attendant courses. By the time they were ready to order dessert, they had learned, roundabout, that their families were on sufficiently comparable economic and social levels; and that they were rapidly coming to like each other very much.

After presenting them with dessert menus, the waiter stood at attention by their table.

"Don't you think cheese and crackers might be best?" Gary asked.

"Mmm, yes," Joyce said. It had been a large meal.

"Roquefort?"

She nodded.

"And how about some brandy and coffee?"

"Mmm."

The waiter had it all down and was off again.

Their patter was resumed and continued through the wedges of cheese and as they sat sipping at coffee and brandy. Anecdotes, a competition to see who had gone to the crazier high school. Stories about eccentric relatives, friends, acquaintances. A light, pleasant flow, not unaided by their cumulative intake of alcohol.

They hadn't finished with their coffees and brandies when the first show started. The pianist who had been playing right along was now reinforced by a bass and drums, and the bassist rather quietly introduced a Miss Susanne Gray. Miss Gray turned out to be a very pretty singer. She did a good long set, well varied. And when they were turned loose, for their choruses on the songs and for one number to themselves, the instrumentalists proved themselves sensitive and competent, individually and as a unit. The pianist had clearly shed his tinkly dinner-music style of the earlier evening and now played some very down-to-earth things. All the performers appeared to be students.

Gary and Joyce had both turned their chairs sideways to catch the show. Now they joined in the firm round of applause as the set ended. There was more reorganization at the bandstand after the applause and bows had ended; Gary's attention was diverted from it by the return of the waiter.

"Would you care for anything else?"

"Joyce, would you like another drink?"

She nodded and smiled.

"Bourbon and water?"

"Fine."

Gary placed the order and redirected his attention to the bandstand. All personnel shifted, and a new group was up, with tenor saxophone and guitar in addition to the previous instrumentation. They started a current slow-tempo tune and couples began getting up from tables to dance in a small area before the stand.

"Dance?" Gary asked.

"Uh-huh," said Joyce.

They were not the last couple out, but the floor was already crowded when they got there. They were lucky in finding a small clear space near the edge.

He was pleased with the ease with which she came into his arms, and with the way she held herself, once there.

They didn't talk while dancing; she put her head down by his shoulder. Several tunes went by pleasantly this way.

Then the guitar moved back from the mike and turned on his pickup. The drums picked up the tempo and it was one of the current rock tunes. Gary and Joyce let go of each other and began doing the fast-dance movements. He didn't suppose that he was very good at them, but he was perhaps a bit tight and Joyce didn't seem to be giving him critical looks.

59

After a couple of the fast ones he suggested a return to the table. There they found their fresh drinks getting warm.

"Oof." Gary mimed fatigue and picked up his glass. Joyce smiled and picked up her own.

Their evening's patter continued as they sipped bourbon and watched the dancers. Their waiter kept an eye on them and was always ready for their reorders.

The band took a break, then came back to start a new set with rock. Gary and Joyce automatically got up and went back to the floor. By now the dancing seemed effortless to him, some instinctive ritual of exorcism. The music went to slow, and she came just a little closer now than before.

They stayed on the floor for the whole set, then went back again to their table and drinks. There was a brief pause.

"Joyce," Gary said, "I remember the other day when I made a joke about the Self-Discipline Plan, you didn't think it was too funny, did you?"

"No, I didn't."

"Does it scare you that much?"

"Yes, it does."

"But why? You're bright—your being here proves that."

"Of course I was admitted here, but so was everyone who's ever . . . really, let's not talk about it."

"Okay." They finished their drinks and ordered another round. The music started again and they danced some more. They returned to the table and picked up their glasses where they'd left off. Then Susanne Gray was coming back.

"Do you want to hear another set of her?" Gary asked. "I thought we could go somewhere else."

"Okay."

Gary caught the waiter and called for the bill, and tried

not to look too horrified when he saw the amount. He was glad he'd brought his checkbook along. With a check written out and cash for the waiter, they left as Susanne Gray was just getting going again.

The corridor outside the Tower Room was relatively silent.

"Where are we going?" Joyce asked.

"I don't know."

"Okay."

They took the elevators down to the shopping floors and window-browsed. There were scattered couples and singles in the halls and visible through the windows of bars and eating places.

"Let's go outside," Gary said.

"Fine."

The outdoor air was a further step down from the crowding and noise of the Tower Room. The stars were clear and bright, the air just a little chilly for the way they were dressed. He offered and she took his arm. With her comfortably up against his side, they crossed the road and began walking at random through the grass.

He supposed he was probably drunk by now. That last round was catching up with him. But it was a fine night, and he had a pretty girl on his arm. He again worried briefly about her worry about the Self-Discipline Plan, but it soon passed out of his mind.

They were into a stand of trees, the huge Tower hidden behind them by branches and trunks. Joyce let herself shiver once, and Gary, perhaps a little slowly, offered her his jacket. She protested. So did he, and she finally accepted. To effect the transfer they had to stop walking. Gary shucked the coat off and carefully put it around her shoulders.

Facing her, he took her gently by his coat and kissed her.

"You're going to freeze without your jacket," she finally said.

"Don't worry," he said.

They walked again. She moved her arm down from his elbow and their hands interlocked.

Before long, unfortunately, he did feel cold, despite his evening's intake, and she noticed it.

"You *are* freezing."

He laughed. "Well, yes."

"Maybe we should be getting inside."

"All right."

She returned his jacket when they got back inside the Tower. The question now was where to go next. He wanted very much to ask her up to his room, but he knew, if hazily, that it wasn't right yet. He looked at his watch.

"What time is it?" she asked.

He told her.

"Maybe I'd better be getting in. I was planning on getting up in the morning. I've got all kinds of work to do."

"Well, then, I guess we'd better head for the elevators."

They rode and walked to her door with their fingers still linked. Nothing was said, but nothing seemed to need to be said. They were high together.

She had unlocked the door.

"Joyce," Gary said, "I'd like to see you again next weekend. Friday night, and Saturday night too if it's okay."

"Okay."

"I'm afraid I can't always spend as much money as I did tonight, but we'll find things to do."

"Sounds fine."

"Good enough." He kissed her again. ". . . Well, g'night."

"G'night." Then she disappeared behind the door.

7

Perhaps a few words here about my own situation and activities during this same time. This was, of course, still before I met Gary.

It was the beginning of my junior year, and I thought I had it. In some ways, I did. My suite was the kind of thing unwindowed frosh dream about. By tradition and with Administration approval and support it was the residential siege of the editor of the *Tumbrel*. Living room, bedroom, kitchen, and bath, all good-sized. Lots of glass frontage. Furnished in Scandinavian modern, enriched by my own touches, which included Picasso and Dali prints, Fisher, Garrard, and KLH components, a fair-sized collection of baroque, jazz, and rock records, a chafing dish, a bar, and a slot-racing set. A couple of other things: one, a rather rare print titled "Strassenbild im Jahre 1900," showing a street scene full of modern transport—moving-belt sidewalks, steam monorails, dirigibles—and of cheerful, red-faced, chubby folk, and dating from 1896. The other was in the bathroom. In order to see just to what extent the Administration would go along with requests I might make, I'd asked for a bidet. They put it in. I doubted that one American college girl in a hundred knew how to use a bidet, and I didn't have many guests anyway. So I went to the five and ten on the shopping floors and got myself some toy boats and tiny submarines that ran on baking powder.

I paid the same rate for that suite as freshmen paid for their cramped roomettes. Such was the practical prestige attached to the editorship of MU's student magazine. This rent was a great boon—others for me were a full-tuition scholarship and generous parents. Almost the only reason why I didn't have a Rolls-Royce was that the University didn't allow students to have motor vehicles. (About the only other things forbidden were marriage and national fraternities.)

At any rate, I was sure I was comfortable. I couldn't really have afforded a Rolls anyway, but I was comfortable —I could eat at the Tower Room as often as I wanted, and I could keep my refrigerator well-stocked with beer.

My world consisted primarily of my suite, my studies, and my work on the magazine. My suite I've described sufficiently. My studies were almost as comfortable. I was taking the general Arts course—the grand old humanities in massive, rigorous doses—and using my elective time to dip into anything else that interested me. My real load was a bit lighter than average because of editorial responsibilities. Credits for that fall term were brought up to acceptability by the addition of Advanced Editorial Workshop, which was a weekly round table in which the editors of all the publications discussed various problems with a professor of journalism who had been on the New York *Times*, had edited a science-fiction pulp, had been managing editor of a car-and-home magazine, and had been a publisher's editor in nonfiction. We learned quite a bit from him, and from one another as well.

Thus dovetailed my studies into my magazine work. This took up a fair amount of time, since we published issues at least twice a quarter, since the editorial staff consisted of me and Patty, and since I still wound up writing great hunks of our material myself. The whole thing was enjoyable, though, from reading brand-new incoming manuscripts and writing my own little slams at the Administration, through reading of proof hot from the University Printshop and the jigsaw puzzle of layout, to the sight of stacks of mint-new copies of an issue ready for distribution —these always got great sighs from both Patty and me.

The *Tumbrel* had started some years before as a humor magazine. When the lit magazine went down under its own weight of self-importance and intramural squabbles, the *Tumbrel* started unobtrusively running straight fiction, poetry, and criticism. The editor just before me, Heath, had begun the continuing trend to making the *Tumbrel* a still more general magazine. He had opened the door to faculty contributions, and had started running book, music, film, and sports columns. My own attempts at further widening our scope had so far been futile—I had once, during the previous year, while still under Heath, run a section of girlie photos, labeled "Girlie Photo Section," featuring local wenches in aspects of undress. We'd had to order another printing of that issue. But the feature had had to be dropped—pretty girls at MU were publicly too modest to allow us further variety, and those who had posed for our cameras complained that their phones were ringing too much. So much for my trail-blazing.

Although I still had notions of scope-expansion, my prime concern for the magazine was competence. "Excellence" was the word I sometimes whispered to myself, but did not dare pretend to. Competence was, for now, goal enough. My one and great helpmeet in its pursuit was Patty, who had first become associated with the magazine the same year as I did, when we were both freshmen. We had both worked under Heath. She had never tried to set any hooks into the editorship, but I knew very well that she could have done my job at least as well as I did it, and still done the assistant's work as well. Although she was extremely attractive, there was never any hint of romance between us, probably because our work-relationship was so good that we never wanted to take any chance of wrecking it. We were like brother and sister, and we both knew that Modern University is not a good place to be an only child.

On top of everything else, I was, in desultory fashion, doing writing not intended for the *Tumbrel*. I had finished my first novel the preceding summer at home, just before having to come up early to get the first fall issue whipped together. The book was now kicking around the offices of who-knew-how-many publishers in New York City—an agent there knew which office it was in when, and I was deeply grateful for being relieved of the burden of keeping track of the script and its status. What I was working on now, though, wasn't intended for publication anywhere. It was strictly private, a project of recollection titled "Who Is Duncan Chase?"—sort of a poor boy's Proust. An attempt to capture, define, figure out—devoid of narrative and probably also of any worth, even to me. Enough about that.

I knew well the therapeutic values of relaxation and recreation, and therefore, despite my heavy schedule, obtained them. My major source of these was my club, a group of male students aiding one another in the quest for relaxation and recreation, who dined and drank together every Wednesday evening and gave parties as a unit. Attendance at club dinners and parties got me regularly out of my shell, allowed me to drink without having to drink alone, let me loosen up in company I knew was getting as loose as I was.

I was not without the company of young ladies either;

there were girls I was seeing. But Patty was my companion at most of the club parties, pretty and charming and my sister. I had had a paramour, Nancy, the preceding year. We were still on speaking terms, but apart from that shared meal her first night back we weren't seeing each other. And I spent too much time wondering if we might possibly get something going again.

But I had my cozy little world, with, as I've said, an occasional guest. I probably knew how artificial it was, but I couldn't have cared. If it ever did get to me, I could always sail my submarines in the bidet.

8

Gary caught himself by chance in his full-length bathroom mirror one morning following his first date with Joyce. He had just finished dressing and was about to head out for breakfast and his early class. He was standing before the mirror for a last quick check, and he caught himself. He almost laughed aloud when he realized that he looked like his own ideal of the College Student. His clothes were part of it—gray crew-neck sweater over a white button-down shirt, dark slacks, loafers with dark socks—and the books and notebook held at his side were part of it, but it was more the face, and not so much the face as the expression. Alert but relaxed, ready to take in information and act appropriately on it. His own Ideal Student. It *was* funny. Then he tore off for breakfast and class.

It was easy enough for him to feel this way. He was less than three weeks into his freshman year. He had received no grades yet. He had had just one date with the girl his pillow represented these nights. The Self-Discipline Plan seemed as near to him and as real as Atlantis or Lemuria.

A little later in the week he decided to get his uniform. He bought the blazer, one of the gray shirts—correct for daytime wear of the uniform—and the proper silk tie striped with black and silver. He shuddered a little as he wrote out his check, then took up the shirt, tie, receipt, and alterations claim-check and went back up to his room to ponder his lack of frugality.

Frazier knocked on Gary's door at six o'clock Friday morning. It had been decided the night before that this morning, for the sheer hell or whatever of it, they would get up early and see how things looked at such an hour.

They were walking around the campus, heading toward the stadium. The sun was just on its way up, leaving the sky pink. Their shoes were covered with a film of dew.

"You've been looking kind of ill at ease lately," Gary was saying. "Don't tell me your grades are down already."

"No, of course not. I don't know. It's just—well, I'm not too comfortable here yet."

"Why not?"

"No real reason, I guess." Frazier frowned at himself. "You've certainly made a fine adjustment, though."

"Why not? This is where I am."

"I suppose." Frazier dug his cigarettes and lighter out of the pockets of his up-collared golf jacket. "I just can't trust the place."

"Self-Discipline?"

"Yeah." The wind blew Frazier's lighter-flame horizontal. "That's part of it."

"But you knew about that before you came here."

"Oh yes. And I suppose I could even see arguing for its utility. But somebody has to run it."

"True."

"And I can't help thinking about what Clark said that day. You know, about 'some of you may think we've tried to give you enough rope.' I wonder if maybe that isn't exactly what it is. Or else why would they make this place such a students' paradise?"

"Why shouldn't students have a paradise like anyone else?"

Frazier snorted. "Since you started this whole discussion by asking me a question, don't go getting funny on me. All I can say for now is that I don't trust this place."

"Is there any place you do trust?"

"Yeah, more or less. Back home. In Detroit I've got a pretty fair idea of what's what. I may not know all the details of the inner circles of politics there and so forth, but at least I know enough of what's going on to get me by."

"And you don't know enough here?"

"Hell, no! I'm going to try to find out, though—if I don't get liquidated first."

Gary grunted. "Look, isn't it possible that the whole thing's on the level—that the faculty and Administration are here for the reasons they say they are, and that the Self-Discipline Plan is run as fairly as possible?"

"Sure it's possible. Can you prove it?"

"Well—no."

"Okay. Come back when you can."

The conversation switched over to football prospects, and soon they went back inside to warm up.

Gary picked up his uniform blazer on the appointed day and took it and the white shoulder tags that came with it up to his room. He tried the outfit on—part way, with a once-worn white shirt to keep the gray one fresh, and with the slacks he had on rather than the exactly right ones.

He struck his Ideal Student pose before his mirror, with

books and notebook in hand. Yes, the white-tagged blazer and the striped tie heightened it. Yes, he thought, an *excellent* adjustment.

He saw Joyce Friday, Saturday, and Sunday of that week.

Friday night supper was considerably more modest than their first meal together. They ate in the second-floor cafeteria, perhaps more comfortably than in the Tower Room. It was cafeteria food, served without wine, and thus left their attention free for each other. They talked easily, swapping anecdotes and idiosyncrasies, not boring each other.

After supper they went to one of the quieter bars and sat over a pitcher. They kept talking, and Joyce drank almost as much of it as Gary did.

They stopped by their rooms for coats and then went outside. It was colder than it had been the preceding weekend. Here, without a background of other people, there seemed less obligation to keep the talk going. They stopped and kissed and he put his hands on her breasts. After a while they went back inside for a few more beers, and at a reasonable hour they wound up kissing again before her door. Then they said good night and she went inside.

Saturday afternoon was warmer than Friday night. They lay on the grass to listen to the away football game. Modern was playing a high-ranked West Coast team and won by a touchdown. The victory was an excuse for starting the day's embraces.

Supper was hamburgers and Cokes at the snackbar. Joyce put her foot down concerning Gary's paying double for meals and insisted on making it dutch. She reassured him that he could pay for the evening's drinks. Which he proceeded to do, as they just had time for two rounds of Bud before their movie started. At the show each offered the other a hand, and they held hands through the picture, interested in the screen action and in no great hurry.

After the show and a few more beers they went outside again. Their embraces were horizontal in the grass. With her coat still on her, he opened her blouse and managed, with difficulty, to unhook her bra. She protested with small negative hums when one of his hands reached the top of her stocking, and he desisted. Their parting activities in her not untrafficked hallway were more limited.

Sunday afternoon he worked manfully to get his studying squared away before the time when he was to meet her for supper. They split a pizza and a small bottle of Chianti in a little place that reminded him of little places back home. They didn't go outside because she had homework she had to do. They kissed and held each other at her door, and then he went back to his room and did more of his advance reading of his texts.

9

The next week swirled by for Gary like a single day. He saw a lot of Joyce, looked forward to seeing more of her over the weekend. Because of a non-jibing of their schedules he took most of his Monday-through-Friday meals in the somewhat less pleasurable company of Frazier and Liebman.

"Art, you know anything about the clubs?" Frazier asked one evening over the tag ends of supper in the cafeteria.

"What about them?"

"What do they do, for instance?"

"They're sort of token eating clubs," Liebman said. "It'd be impractical for them to eat together all the time, so they meet each Wednesday night for a big meal and a business meeting."

"Are they like fraternities?" Gary asked. He was aware of the existence of the clubs, if only through his orientation folder, but hadn't yet given them much thought.

"A little," Liebman said. "They give parties and so forth, and they host their alumni at homecoming. But they don't have any pins or pledging."

"How do you get in?" said Frazier.

"You're invited," said Liebman.

"Oh."

"How many people are in these things?" Gary asked.

"Oh, maybe half of all male students—about a thousand, I guess."

"Aren't there any for female students?" said Frazier.

"Uh-uh. The girls generally seem to prefer organizations within their majors and the clubs are strictly social."

"How many clubs are there?" Gary said.

"About twenty-five, I think. Tower is best, Compass is pretty good, and the rest come after that."

"I knew there had to be a hierarchy," Frazier said. "I suppose they've got some kind of overall governing body, too."

"No, there's nothing they really do in common. They just try to maintain cordial relations on an individual basis."

Frazier grunted.

"What are the rules govering them?" Gary asked.

"There aren't any. The three of us could form one right now if we wanted to. Getting together the money for big parties might be something else again."

"Yeah," said Frazier.

"But really," Liebman went on, "so long as a club doesn't damage University property or get caught doing anything flagrantly illegal, the Administration couldn't care less what it does. Nor could the other clubs."

"Are they expensive?" Gary asked.

"Not really. You pay for your meals and for what you and your date drink at a party."

"Sounds great."

"I don't know," Frazier said. "You can do about as well on your own, I should think."

Liebman shrugged. "If you want to. If you know people who are giving parties."

"Still sounds good," Gary said.

In the evenings Gary and Joyce studied together. He was able to cover his regular assignments during the daytime hours between classes, and so was spending these evenings on reading ahead in his texts, doing corollary reading from other sources, or working well ahead on long-term projects.

Joyce was almost as well up as he was, but still insisted on studying faithfully Sunday through Thursday evenings. Gary respected her perhaps not unhealthy fear of the Self-Discipline Plan, and remained well-behaved. They did, however, allow a half-hour out of each of these study-dates for extensive good-night sayings.

They'd stand in front of her door, chattering between embraces, and playing games like Slap Joyce's Rump or Tickle Gary's Ribs. They got their work done too.

That weekend brought the first home football game. Gary wore his new uniform, gray shirt and all.

"Well!" Joyce said when she opened her door and saw him. "You look good in the uniform."

"Thanks. You're looking pretty fine yourself. You really think the uniform is okay?"

"Fine."

So he bowed to her and she curtsied to the extent that her suit's straight skirt would allow, and then they started toward the stadium.

He had with him a couple of rolls of toilet paper to throw as streamers. He'd been meaning to lift them from the floor supply room, the place where you got such refills, along with light bulbs and cleaning supplies. But then this morning the Floor Supervisor had come down the hall, passing out two rolls at each room. Enthusiasm was apparently expected.

They boarded a passing elevator and found it jammed. Gary was encouraged by the sight of two other young men in uniforms, and by the fact that no one seemed to take notice of his, nor of his white shoulder tags.

The first-floor arcade was crowded with students, mostly in couples, with a good proportion of the males wearing uniforms. Everybody was flowing out the front doors, and Gary and Joyce found that the only speed they could move at was that of the pack. This was acceptable, as everyone was heading for the stadium and they were on time.

Along the way he spotted one instance of the uniform that confused him. It was worn by a man who seemed to be in his early thirties, and his shoulder tags were gold. He remarked on this to Joyce and they decided that a uniform with gold tags must be the mark of the faithful alumnus.

It was perfect weather for football, cold but with a clear sky and all outdoors in Kodachrome color. Program vendors, situated along the cement walk from Tower to stadium, were doing a brisk business. So were pom-pom sellers and girls with great bunches of huge white flowers with black M's painted on them. Gary bought a program and a pom-pom, one of its hemispheres of black crepe paper, the other of silver. He bought one of the painted flowers—somehow they reminded him of souvenir turtles —and had to stop to fumble to get it pinned to the jacket of Joyce's tweed suit.

He was noticing more of the gold-tag uniforms now as they went along and considered that the alumni turnout must be pretty good. He wondered what Homecoming would be like.

He surrendered their tickets at the gate and got half of each back. Before going to their seats they stopped at an

78

inside concession stand. He got a "Beat the Irish" button for himself—Frazier had made himself a cardboard button saying "Beat Our Lady," but that was perhaps a little too much. He bought caramel corn and pop-top Buds for Joyce and himself—the price here was a nickel a can higher than in the Tower. There was a sign over the concession stand: "Please Do Not Throw Beer Cans."

They found their way to their seats in the freshman section, the end zone. The stadium was filling fast. There was a large contingent in the visitors' stands, including a pep band that was not about to allow the crowd to go long without music.

Gary suggested to Joyce that there would probably not be much time later to devote to their beers, so they opened their cans now. *Pst, pst,* and they were sitting there in the confusion they'd brought with them, sipping beer while juggling the pom-pom and both looking at the program.

Before long, it got started. The MU band trotted in, with black uniforms laden with silver braid, followed by leaping cheerleaders. There was quick marching, the familiar victory song addressed to the visitors, more marching, twirlers tossing batons high into the air, then relative order with the band formed at the center of the field and the crowd standing for the National Anthem and the raising of the flag. With everyone still standing, the MU alma mater came next. Gary and Joyce followed the lyrics in the program. Her voice was high, clear, and slightly off key. His baritone was a little farther off, but good and loud. Then there was the MU fight song, cheering, and then the band took its seats and everybody sat down again.

The starting line-ups were announced, visitors and defenders cheered by their respective factions. The kick-off was decided—MU receiving—and the crowd stood to hold up its thumbs and go "sssssssssss*BOOM!*"

It was a hard, fast game. Both teams were strong on offense and there was no stagnation. Neither side showed too much hesitation about fouling, and scores grew rapidly.

Joyce was frantic, outshouting Gary, who was himself going wild. Singing, shouting, waving pom-poms, and tossing toilet paper served as emotion outlets for the cool young men in black and silver down on the field. They might as well tear out the seats, Gary thought, we spend more time standing then sitting. MU touchdowns won him emphatic if badly aimed kisses from Joyce. The noise in the stadium would have frightened anyone who didn't know what was going on.

He remembered the story from *This Side of Paradise* of Burne Holiday and Phyllis Styles at the Harvard-Princeton game—indicative of anti-rah-rah as early as 1916 (he thought that must have been the year). And now back to the other side of the circle, and rah-rah appeared as relief, the inexpensive drug of the undergraduates. Enthusiasm seemed to be expected, and he could begin to see its uses.

The MU band put on a fine show at halftime, songs current and marching precise, giving Gary's throat a rest. Then the game started again. Gary was sure he couldn't shout any more, but he did. There were airhorns and trumpets in the stands to support the calls of the crowd.

It looked like it was going to be a tie. But MU got the ball and kept it, and there was an eighty-yard run, giving a touchdown in the last five seconds. A damn fine game.

Everybody was standing and there was shouting and last rolls of toilet paper being tossed and Joyce was hugging him and screaming happily into his ear. Then everybody started leaving. Hanging on to her hand, he led the way down over the bleachers and out. She took his arm and held it tight to her for the walk back to the Tower. They headed for one of the smaller bars for celebratory beers.

The place was crowded and noisy; everybody was laughing, and the fight song and alma mater were being played over and over again on the jukebox. Gary and Joyce got a pitcher and a table as much out of the way as possible. For a while he couldn't stop talking about that last rush. "Did you see how—" and so forth. Joyce smiled and nodded, looking at him as if he'd been the ball-carrier.

Then he stopped and they sat without talking.

"What are you thinking?" she finally asked.

He'd begun to lose the euphoria of shameless rah-rah and had been thinking again about the damn paramour business. "I was wondering where we ought to go for supper."

"It's up to you."

He laughed. "Thanks. Keith was telling me about a place he's 'discovered.' He says it's inexpensive but very pleasant."

"Okay."

"Good enough." He glanced at his watch. "No hurry, though. Let's see what we can do with the rest of the pitcher."

What they did was finish it. Then they went window-shopping through the store floors, walking aimlessly with scores of others, all still somewhat exhilarated with the game.

Dinner was taken at Frazier's restaurant, dutch as usual. It was quiet and the food was good, and Gary relaxed and tried to put the burning issue of formalization out of his mind.

"Where to now?" Joyce asked as they left the restaurant. It wasn't a bad question. They'd seen the current movie the night before, doubling with Frazier and a girl named Kathy, and this was one of the few evenings with no other events.

"Well, we could go to a bar, or we could buy some

lighter fluid and go out and burn anthills. Or if you think you can trust me, I've got most of a bottle of bourbon back in my room."

"Well . . . I *guess* I can trust you."

He cackled for her like a melodrama villain, then gave her his arm and they were off for his room.

"I like the picture," she said. She'd gotten glimpses of the Buffet a couple of times before when he'd stopped off for a coat or jacket, but now she was sitting on his sofa and this was her first opportunity for a long look at the print.

"Do you?" Gary was in the bathroom mixing drinks with the ice-cold tap water. "That's good. You should have seen the look the girl at the Art Center gave me when I bought it."

"Really, it's almost funny in this context."

"I guess that's why I bought it."

She smiled as she took the drink he handed her.

"But I do think it's a cheerful touch. Kind of livens up the old Winter Palace."

"Uh-huh."

"What do you think of the place?"

"Actually, it's just the same as my room—physically, I mean. The picture really *is* good, your radio looks functional, and you've got some variety on your bookshelves. I approve."

"That's good. I'll have to see yours sometime."

"Okay."

He sat in his desk chair sipping his drink while she sipped at hers and looked through his bookshelves in more detail, occasionally taking a book down and glancing at its blurbs and first few pages.

"I'm going to have to borrow some of these from you sometime."

"Sure," he said. "Anything you like."

"Not right now, though. I've got too much work to do."

"Any time . . . Say, how about some music?"

"Good idea."

He found the soft-music station on the radio. They committed the unpardonable offense of actually listening to the background music, while they slowly finished off their drinks.

"Do you want a refill?" He stood up in case of an affirmative reply.

"Not right away." She set her glass on one of the shelves above the sofa.

He put his down on the desk and sat down next to her on the sofa. "Good game today, huh?"

"Wonderful. Thanks." She touched the flower still pinned to her suit jacket.

"That's okay. We *must* go all out to support the team."

She smiled and came easily into his arms. Soon they were lying together on the sofa, holding each other tight with the music still playing softly.

"I'm afraid," he whispered, "we're crushing your whatsis flower."

He released her and she sat up to take off the jacket and put it over the back of the desk chair.

"Better now?"

"Well, now that you mention it, the press of my uniform isn't exactly being aided here." He stood up to remove his blazer and tie and lay them carefully across his desk, then returned to his position on the sofa. "Okay?"

"Well, I don't know. You're practically half naked now."

"Shall I do a couple of Tarzan yells for you?"

"That's all right." She lay down again beside him, and they were holding each other once more.

Then a little later he unbuttoned her blouse, and it

went from there. There were murmurings, little questions and answers. And then, rather than just proceed and hope for tacit agreement, he asked her to stay for the night.

"Please, Gary, no. I'm afraid we're going too fast already."

"Okay." He kissed her on the lips, very lightly now. Then they lay there quietly, still holding together tightly. The music from the radio seemed inconsequential.

He kissed her mouth, lightly and repeatedly, each time with just a little less contact and motion. "Would you like another drink now?"

"Yes."

He patted her fanny, then got up to get the glasses, the bottle, and the ice-water from the bathroom. They sat together on the sofa to have their drinks. She'd put herself back together while he'd made them, and now she sat with her legs folded up under her and with her head on his shoulder between sips. There seemed to be no need of talk.

After they'd finished their drinks and sat there for a while longer, he looked at his watch. "Guess I'd better be getting you in soon."

"Okay."

They got up from the sofa. She put her jacket with the half-crushed flower back on, he his tie and blazer. He lent her his comb so that she could reorganize her hair, then straightened out his own a bit.

"All set?"

"Mmm-hmm," she said, giving a final straightening to her skirt.

He gathered up the program and pom-pom for her to take, and they left the room. They said their usual long good night at her door, and then he went back to his room, put the bottle back where it belonged on the shelf, rinsed out the glasses they'd used, and went to bed.

There had been no prearrangements for the next day, and he didn't call her. He supposed he was being petty but he didn't much care. He got in a lot of studying that afternoon.

That evening he didn't feel like trying to push farther ahead on academics. He wound up getting out his complimentary copy of the *Tumbrel* and reading a few of the pieces he hadn't had time for before. Then he got out his typewriter and paper and set up shop on his desk. This (with his corrections) is what he wrote:

I went down to Ferd's room to get some Physical Biochemistry 3995 notes. I'd missed the lecture because of my next-door neighbor's funeral. I knocked, the door opened, and there was Ferd in his black fez.

"Hi," said Ferd, holding up a gallon jug. "Want some?"

Not wanting to hurt his feelings, I took five pulls. "Chivas Regal again, eh?"

"Yeah," said Ferd. "How's your mono?"

"About the same," I said, coughing blood onto my handkerchief to show him.

"Oh," said Ferd. "Well, come on in."

"Thanks," I said, and went inside. The phonograph was playing "Gloomy Sunday."

"This is Herb," said Ferd. "Herb lives across the hall."

Herb stood squarely in the middle of the room, wearing a red-tagged uniform and smoking a meerschaum. "Hi there," he said, and gave me an uncomfortably firm handshake.

"How do you do," I said.

"Herb is actually a goddam bastard," said Ferd. "He only acts like a goddam bastard to fool you."

Then I looked at my watch. "I've got to take another pill," I said.

"Sure," said Ferd.

"Where can I get some water?"

"Bathroom," said Ferd, trying to find it to point it out to me.

When I got to the bathroom, there was a beautiful girl standing there naked, gargling.

"What's your name?" I said.

"Rrrrrrrrg," she said.

"Russian?"

"No," she said. "It's Cecilia."

"You smell of popcorn," I said. "That is a wholesome smell." I kissed her. "You taste of mouthwash. You are a wholesome girl."

"Okay, where do you want to do it?"

"Don't be so middle-class," I said.

"Why are you coughing blood?" she asked.

"I always do," I said.

"Oh," she said.

I took my pill.

Back in the other room, Herb was still standing as he had been. Ferd had passed out across his desk. I looked out the window.

"Sure is dark out there," I said, shivering.

"It usually is, this time of night," said Herb.

A train went by.

"I didn't know the Rutland was still running through here," I said.

"It never did." Herb blew a smoke ring.

An apelike young man came in without knocking and went into the bathroom.

"I'm going to wake Ferd," I said. "I need some lecture notes."

"You want to borrow Ferd's notes?"

"Yes. He takes very good notes. I know because I sat next to him when I was in class."

"Even so, you can't borrow them. Every evening when he comes back to the room he burns the day's notes." Herb pointed to a charred spot in the middle of the carpet.

"Oh," I said. Then I wanted to change the subject. "Whose is Cecilia?"

"She was here when Ferd got the room."

"Oh," I said, and then I had to cough some more.

"What's the matter?" said Herb politely.

"I tell everyone it's mono. Actually, I've been given six months. I count the days."

"I'll bet you do."

"Only six months," I said, and I knew that I had that same silly smile on my face again.

"Some would say you're lucky," said Herb. "But of course *I'm* not one of those who would."

Ferd, who had waked when a coal from Herb's pipe had landed on the back of his neck, said "Yes, you are."

Herb placed a thumb in one of Ferd's eye sockets and gently told him to be quiet. Ferd pushed him away.

"You pose very well, Herb, but you never did fool me. I know that—"

Ferd stopped talking when Herb hit him over the head with an ashtray. It had been made from a Coke bottle, softened and then flattened and finally turned up at the edges. It broke and pieces of it went all over the floor.

"Cecilia!" Herb shouted toward the bathroom. "Bring a broom and dustpan."

"Not now! I'm with Max from down the hall."

"When you get to it, then."

I thought I should say something. "They say another war is inevitable. Maybe it'll help."

"I don't need it," said Herb.

I looked him over again, comparing his perfectly arranged red-tagged uniform with my simple breechclout. "Maybe not," I said.

"No," said Herb. "I don't need excuses like you and Ferd and all the others."

"All the others except Cecilia," I said. "She's too stupid and much too beautiful."

"True," said Herb, then looked at his watch. "Excuse me."

Herb went into the bathroom and Cecilia came out with a broom and dustpan.

"I don't get it," she said. "Every hour on the hour he—"

"I don't want to hear about it," I shouted quickly. "Don't worry about it. You don't have to. Say, you wouldn't be taking Physical Biochemistry 3995, would you?"

Later that evening I went to the regular mixer. From the meatline I picked a thin platinum blonde with a cast in one eye to dance with.

The music was slow. I held her close and tried not to cough into her ear.

"Whatsyourmajor," she said.

"Oh, come now," I said.

"Whereyoufrom," she said.

"You meet the weirdest girls at these dances."

"Whatflooryouon."

"You aren't a student here, are you?"

"My father's dean of the College of Microcinematography. You wanna make something of it?"

"No," I said. "How old are you?"

"Twelve," she said. "Whatsa matter? Age of consent is ten in this state."

"Sorry," I said. "I'd forgotten." We danced some more.

"You got some money?" she asked.

"Yes," I said.

"Enough to take me to the Tower Room?"

"No."

"Thanks for the dance," she said, and walked away.

"Thank *you*," I said, bowing.

Then I danced for a while with a girl with two broken legs.

After coming back from taking a pill, I ran into Cecilia. We danced for a while, then I gave in, and we finally did it in my room. Afterwards, we were amusing ourselves, lying there on my sofa looking at each other's ID's.

"Mmmm," said Cecilia finally, "let's go up to the Tower Room."

"Can't," I said. "I've only got fifteen cents."

"Christ!" said Cecilia, and got up from the sofa and walked out of the room.

"Wait!" I said. "You forgot your ID."

I didn't stay long in the room by myself. The ticking of the twenty clocks, which I usually enjoyed, made me nervous, and the guy across the hall was being ill and had left his door open. Coughing, I picked up a worn pocket edition of *Decline and Fall of the Roman Empire* and went to the nearest bar.

The beer I got with my last fifteen cents was flat, as usual. "Gloomy Sunday" was playing and Gibbon had lost his sparkle. I noticed a couple copulating to one side of the jukebox and thought of Cecilia.

I went back to Ferd's room. He had passed out across the desk again. Herb's full uniform lay on the floor, and the window was wide open. Cecilia was in the bathroom.

"Cecilia," I said.

"Rrrrrrrg," she said.

"Cecilia," I said, "I love you. I've only got six months to live and I want to spend every minute of that brief time with you."

"Christ!" said Cecilia.

"I guess I've put it wrong. Cecilia, let's be paramours."

I held out my copy of Gibbon, offering it as my favour. She took it and, in return, gave me her bottle of mouthwash. She took my hand and we ran to the *Daily Bulletin* offices to make sure the announcement would appear in the next day's paper. From there went back to my room.

Then it was seven in the morning. Cecilia and I went outside and watched the sun rise over the Power Plant. I coughed very little.

"I'm hungry," said Cecilia.

So we went back to the Tower for breakfast.

End

By the time he was finished with it, Gary had a title for the thing. He carefully inked in "Life in the Tower Is as Good as Anywhere Else" at the top of the first sheet, and put his name, room number, and phone number on it.

From the directory he got the room number of the *Tumbrel* office. It was ten-thirty. He went to the office and slipped his typescript into the mail slot.

10

Gary studied with Joyce as usual the next night. Neither mentioned their lack of contact on Sunday. They studied together the following night as well. Gary was relieved to be able to hide in his books, rather than sit and be obviously silent and thus indicate his growing dread of Paramours' Day, which was this coming Saturday.

They had been planning to study together Wednesday night as well, but shortly before he was to meet her he got an unexpected telephone call.

"Gary Fort?"

"Yes."

"Gary, this is Duncan Chase from the *Tumbrel*. I've read the story you submitted and I'd like to talk to you about it, if you don't mind."

"Sure."

"Could you come up sometime this evening?"

"I guess so."

"Fine. The number's twenty-one hundred. Just come on over. I expect to be in all evening."

"Okay. I can be over in about half an hour, if that's all right."

"Fine. At your convenience."

"Thank you."

"It's nothing. So long for now."

"So long."

He clicked the hook to get a dial tone and called Joyce's number.

"Hi," she said. "What is it?"

"Well, I hope you won't mind, but I just got a call from Duncan Chase, that guy from the *Tumbrel*. You know that story I told you about? Well, he wants me to come over tonight to discuss it."

"That's wonderful."

"That's what I was hoping you'd say. I'm afraid I already told him I'd be over. So I can't meet you, at any rate not when we'd planned."

"That's all right. Do you really think he wants to use the story?"

"I don't know. I hope so—he might want me to do some revision first."

"Uh-huh. Well, I'm very proud of you. Don't worry about me. I'll be seeing you tomorrow night at least, won't I?"

"Sure."

"Fine, then. And call me when you get back in tonight, or come over if it's not too late."

"Okay . . . I'd better get going now."

"Okay. Let me know what happens."

"Will do. Bye for now."

"Bye."

He put the phone down and sat, wondering what this Duncan Chase was expecting. Deciding to play it safe, he got up and changed into his uniform.

He arrived at the door marked 2100, knocked on it, and it opened. He found himself facing the young man he'd heard at the convocation, now wearing chinos and a sweater.

"I'm Gary Fort."

"Of course. Come in."

And thus I began to enter the story.

Gary was impressed with my suite. He hadn't known until now what an upperclassman's residence could be like, hadn't seen one like this in person, at any rate.

We talked for a while about "Life in the Tower." I hadn't much to say about it really, beyond telling him how and when we might use it. I'd simply wanted to meet the author of such a thing, thinking he might be a kindred spirit. As it worked out, he was, to a great extent. This was one of those occasions when the ice breaks easily and you find yourself talking with someone you've just met as if you'd been friends for years.

We talked about a freshman's first impressions of MU. He gave me details rather than trying to make generalizations. It turned out that our families' homes were within a half-hour's drive, and that we knew a couple of the same bars.

He asked to see the rest of the suite, and the bidet got the right kind of laugh out of him. I kept the beers coming and finally I got my plywood-mounted slot-racing track out of the bedroom closet and set it up in the living room. Although he'd had no experience of the kind before, he was good with the little cars, doing almost as well with the clumsy Corvette as with the agile Jaguar.

We finally stopped to let the cars cool off and sat down again with our beers to talk.

"What's the real story on this Paramours' Day?" he asked.

"Huh? Oh, it's the one spot of sentimental fluff on the term calendar, unless you want to count Homecoming. No, it's just supposed to be a convenient day for declarations, to make it a little easier."

"It doesn't seem to be making it any easier for me."

93

I laughed. "I know what you mean."

"What's being paramours supposed to mean? I mean, apart from being a publicly recognized couple."

"Hell, it means something a bit different to everybody. It doesn't matter what it means to me—or to you, for that matter. What matters is what it means to your girl."

"Yeah. Wish I knew."

"You won't know until she's your paramour." I spread my hands. "It could be anything from acceptability for a sleeping arrangement to whole-hog romance."

"I'm afraid it's probably more the second than the first."

"Uh-huh. Is that what you want?"

"I don't know."

I laughed again. "I guess you'll just have to play it by ear—the way all of us do."

He grunted. "Do you have a paramour?"

"Had one once. It's really not all that bad."

"If I thought it was, I wouldn't be in such a quandary now."

I nodded.

"Guess I'll have to wait and see. Can't help feeling scared, though."

"Maybe you shouldn't be making such a big thing of it. I don't know." I didn't have anything like the ex-cathedra feeling I'd expected to have. It was just as well.

"Maybe I'd better be getting along now. I've got an eight o'clock."

I nodded again. "By the way, if you've got some free time tomorrow afternoon, why don't you stop by the office? We're just getting out an issue—that's why we couldn't give attention to your story any sooner than this —and anyhow, you can see us in as close to action as we ever get."

"Okay."

"Good. And if you could bring along some more of your stuff, I'd like to see it."

"I've got drawers full."

"That's what I thought. Let's see it."

He left and I went to pack up my slot-racers.

"What happened?" Joyce asked him when he called her.

"Well, they want to use the story."

"Wonderful. When do I get to see it?"

"They've got the only copy. I'll see if I can get you one soon."

"Okay. I'm getting impatient. What's the great Duncan Chase like?"

"Seems like a pretty decent guy—it was kind of funny. I figured it'd be safest to wear my uniform, so when he opened the door he was wearing a sweater and a pair of chinos."

"Uh-huh."

"But the suite he's got—you've got to see it. Big. And a slot-racing set and a refrigerator full of beer. And the bidet —he was telling me he asked for one to be put in, just as a joke. And they gave it to him. It does crowd things a bit in the bathroom, but there it is."

She laughed easily. "Sounds like I'll have to meet him."

"Definitely. He asked me to stop by the office tomorrow afternoon—wants to see more of my stuff."

"I've got classes all tomorrow afternoon, but see if you can arrange to take me along sometime, okay? You can tell me all about the office tomorrow night."

"Right. Well, I'd better be getting to bed. See you tomorrow."

"See you tomorrow. G'night."

"G'night."

"Patty, there's a freshman coming in sometime this afternoon. I want to see what you think of him. He's the one who wrote that 'Life in the Tower' thing."

"Okay."

"I want to give him a good look at the operation. All this proof sitting around should seem very official."

"What's the upshot?"

"I want to get him to do some more stuff for us. And I've been thinking about expanding the actual staff."

"Good idea." She frowned at the pile of proofs on her desk.

"Yeah, I think it's about time, the way things pile up on us. Anyhow, I think Gary'd be a good prospect—I'd like to at least try him for a while—so be sure to treat him well when he comes in."

"Okay."

I retired to my own desk and we both got back to the tremendously exciting task of proofreading.

Gary came in around three, was introduced to Patty, and was given a tour of our one-room "offices" by me. He seemed especially interested in the mechanics of our publication, spent several moments studying the scaled-down dummy layout on the wall. He'd brought a small pile of manuscripts, which I took with a promise to read them over the weekend. "After all," I said, "Paramours' Day is no problem to me."

"Don't rub it in."

Patty laughed.

I ignored her. "Gary, we've been thinking about reorganizing a bit. It's gotten so that the thing's a little too big for just Patty and me to handle. How'd you like to join up with us—on a mutual trial basis, if you'd like."

"Well . . ."

"I'll tell you, there's a plum coming up. The all-frosh issue will have a freshman editor. Sometimes there's competition for the spot, sometimes there isn't. But you get the idea."

"Yes . . . Okay. Where do I sign?"

"We've got this big black book, and you have to use your blood for ink. No, when would you like to start?"

"Maybe not till after this weekend."

I nodded. "Yeah, I hope you get it settled by then. Okay, Monday afternoon, then?"

"Good enough."

"Okay." We shook hands. "We'll be wrapping up this issue soon, and sometime next week we'll be starting on the next. There's sort of a vacation between issues, so that'll be a good time to get you oriented."

"Fine."

"I think you'll enjoy it. Well, I'd better get back to work. And I promise to read your scripts by Monday."

"No rush."

"Okay then, we'll see you Monday."

"Right."

He said his good-days to Patty and me and was gone.

"What do you think?" I asked.

"He's not bad looking."

"He's already got enough trouble that way. I mean for the magazine."

"Okay, I guess. We'll see."

"True. I think he'll be all right."

That evening, at dinner with Joyce, Gary found it easiest to keep talking about the *Tumbrel*.

"What's the office like?" Joyce asked.

"It looks very functional. A couple of desks and chairs, a couple of phones, some filing cabinets. There's a little mock-up of the next issue on one wall, and framed illustrations on the others."

"And they want you to work with them?"

"As a general office boy, I suppose, but it's my best chance of getting the editorship of the frosh issue."

"Are you sure you have the time?"

"Hell, yes. I'm way ahead in all my courses already. It's about time I had something to relieve the boredom."

"Oh, do I bore you?"

"Don't be silly."

"Okay."

"Where to from here?" he asked when they'd finished.

"Well . . . I was thinking how much you've spent on me so far for drinks. So today I bought a bottle. We could go up to my room."

"But you don't have to feel obligated that way."

"Really, I wanted to. How about it?"

"Sure, if you insist."

So they went to her room. It was almost identical to his. She had a Miro print instead of his Buffet. Gary stared at it while she fixed drinks in the bathroom.

"I think I like it," he said when she came back. "I can't figure out why, but I think I like it."

She smiled and handed him his drink, then turned on the radio.

They sat on the sofa and he tried to keep talking. He was sure that she was as aware as he was of what tomorrow was. They had a few drinks and a few embraces. It got late and she went to sleep in his arms. He managed to get up without waking her, found a blanket to put over her, then went to his own room to sleep.

II

Paramours' Day. Distant football on the grass across from the Tower, with other couples also taking up what was perhaps the year's last dose of sun. Gary and Joyce avoided the most obvious topic of the day, although there were occasionally remarks of humor, intended to probe.

Listening to the away game, he lay on his back or propped up on an elbow with her beside him. He thought that this was the way it should always be, leisurely and sun-drenched.

MU scored a touchdown and Gary, in parody of in-stadium excitement, rolled over to kiss Joyce, then rolled back to continue his contemplation of the high clouds.

MU won again, as the clouds were thickening. Gary and Joyce slowly got up and gathered in their radio, blanket, and the paper cups they'd had Cokes in.

They went inside, separating to change out of their grassing clothes for dinner. Gary went up to his room, set the radio on his desk and the blanket on the sofa. He was long on time until they were to remeet, and sat down at the desk.

On it were letters from high school classmates. He'd been getting more and more lax in his correspondence lately. It was a simple enough swapping of freshman reactions, but all of his pivoted around the Self-Discipline Plan, and that he couldn't discuss with his old friends— there just wasn't the basis for comparison. He'd have to think of ways to answer the letters sometime. If he waited a good while to do so, their authors would think twice about bothering to write him again. Already he was able to predict a lonely Christmas vacation, but for Joyce in Mamaroneck and Duncan in Chappaqua. But who could know if Joyce would even be speaking to him by then? He hoped she would be.

With a little snarl of mock disgust, he got up from the chair and began dressing for the evening. The uniform, he thought—it was, after all, a local holiday of sorts. He fixed his tie with his favorite tack, a small irregular chip of semi-demi-precious stone. A neat, modest favour to offer, if it came to that. Some of his classmates, he thought, would be or were already pledging fraternities, and would wake up mornings to find themselves pinned.

He checked himself in the mirror: the Ideal Student, perhaps about to enter into a miniature marriage. Catch that nervous look in the eyes? He made himself laugh, then left the room to go meet Joyce for dinner.

They ate at the quiet little place that had been Frazier's discovery. More was said with their eyes than with their mouths, and Gary realized that he knew what was going to happen tonight. They sat in a not uncomfortable silence over their brandies and coffees, and when they had finished, he suggested the Tower Room.

"Are you sure you can afford it?"

"I think so, since we've already had dinner."

She smiled and they went up to the top floor.

They got a table and were in good time for the first show, local talent again, a team of one male and one female with songs and patter.

Gary and Joyce drank bourbon and danced and said very little. Then the second show was about to start.

"Do you want to stay for it?" Gary asked.

"Not if you don't want to."

"Well . . . I thought we could try to kill off that bottle in my room."

"Okay."

So she was on his sofa again while he mixed drinks in the bathroom. Maybe one more, he thought, then it would be easy enough to broach the topic.

They sat with their glasses, the radio playing, each trying to ignore the war of nerves.

Finally Gary looked at his watch. "Eleven-twenty. Not much left of today."

"No."

"Well, before it's too late . . ." He removed his little tie tack and held it out to her. "I don't know if it's exactly what a 'favour' is supposed to be, but will you take it?"

"Yes." She took the chip of stone from his hand and fastened it to her dress, and then removed from the dress a tiny pin representing a salamander and held it out to Gary.

He took it and pinned it to his shirt, and then they were grappling feverishly.

"Joyce, is it all right? . . . Stay with me?"

"Uh-huh."

And soon they were helping each other undress. Their favours, so tenderly offered and accepted, lay somewhere in the pile of clothing on the desk chair. The thought Gary was trying to get out of his mind was *now that I've paid the going price.*

He had to leave the sofa for a moment to rummage in a

desk drawer for the prophylactic he knew was there somewhere.

"What are you doing?"

"Trying to find something. Sorry about the interruption,
but I'm afraid it's necessary."

"No, it isn't. I've been on the pills since the start of the
term. They supply them free. Didn't you know that?"

"No."

He went back to the sofa.

It was his first time, and not quite what he'd been expecting. But then, everybody said it never was. It was her
first time too, and that scared him. But he tried to remember all kinds of things that he'd read and been told and did
his best.

"It wasn't too bad, was it?"

"It hurt."

"I know. But it won't again."

"I know."

"You musn't expect too much the first time."

She nodded, then squeezed him.

A little later they tried again.

"That was better, wasn't it?"

"Mmmm."

And finally they went to sleep, a little crowded on the
sofa-bed (which he'd finally pulled out), but not minding
at all.

He woke up when he heard water running. "Joyce?"

"Good morning, darling," she called from the bathroom.

"Morning, honey. Nothing wrong, is there?"

"I don't think so. A little tender."

"That should clear up in a day or so, shouldn't it?"

"I think so." She came out of the bathroom in bra and panties, bent down to kiss him.

He did a little tiger-growl and pulled her onto the bed with him.

"Mph. You men. Just one thing on your minds."

"Don't tell me girls don't think about it too."

"I still haven't stopped since last night." She kissed him again. "But we've got to get some breakfast."

"Ah, the ever-practical female. Okay, give me a crack at the bathroom and then we'll get something to eat."

She got up off the bed and started looking for her slip. He got out of the bed, quickly put the covers back over it. A little self-conscious about his nakedness while she was half dressed, he ducked into the shower and washed himself as rapidly as possible. After toweling himself he decided on an electric shave for time's sake, although he preferred using the lather and blade.

When he came out of the bathroom with his towel wrapped around his waist, she was fully dressed and tidying up the room for him. He crammed the past day's shirt and underwear into the laundry bag in the closet, then pawed through the drawers of the lowboy for fresh linen.

"You're really an atrocious housekeeper," she was saying.

"At least I usually manage to keep the mess out of sight."

"That won't do. When was the last time you vacuumed this carpet?"

"Oh, nineteen twenty-three, I think. Don't worry about it." He pulled his clothes on as rapidly as possible. She, of course, was wearing what she had been wearing the night before so he got into uniform again. "All set."

"Good." She tiptoed up to kiss him once more and then they went out for breakfast.

"Remind me to call the paper tonight," he said between munches of toast, "to get the announcement in."

"Uh-huh," she said, smiling at him and embracing him with her eyes.

He smiled back and continued his attack on the piece of toast. Ever since his shower he'd had in the back of his mind a snatch of a very old oldie, something about "We'll make the best of it."

In the afternoon of that same day, Nancy came to see my new suite for the first time. She came without warning, although I'd invited her several times before to come up for a look. I was not a little surprised to see her at my door.

"You kept asking me if I'd like to see the new place. Today I thought I would."

"Sure. Come in."

She came in and I held up my hand to indicate the living room as a whole. We stood there. I watched her slowly taking it in.

"Very nice," she said. "Lots of windows."

I nodded.

She began walking about the room, appraising it, putting a passing hand on the upholstery.

"May I get you a drink?"

"Okay."

I moved to the bar and quickly made her a gimlet the way she'd always liked them.

"Thank you."

I put together bourbon and soda for myself, stood with it as she continued her tour of the room. She stopped before the amplifier, looking intently at its controls. She ran a hand along a shelf of books, as if their spines were in Braille.

"Do you approve?"

She nodded. "May I see the rest?"

"Of course." I opened the bedroom door. She put her head in long enough to see the windows and the huge double bed with its built-in headboard.

"Uh-huh."

I opened the bathroom door. She couldn't help laughing when she saw the bidet.

"I never thought they'd put it in when I asked for it."

She was still laughing, now through her nose. "I'm sure you've been able to find people to use it for you."

"Not really. I use it myself." I opened the medicine cabinet to show her the plastic boats and submarines.

"Really, Duncan." The way she spoke was an unmitigated laugh.

"Kitchen's next," I said. There she saw the up-to-date appliances and the dirty dishes in the sink.

"I do them at least once a week," I said.

"Very good." She opened the refrigerator, revealing a good stock of little- or no-preparation foods, including a supply of TV dinners, and much beer. "Just want to make sure you're eating well."

"Of course. Lots of food value in beer."

"Of course."

We went back to the living room. She sat down on the sofa.

"You haven't seen the *pièce de résistance* yet. Just a minute." I went and got the race-board out of the bedroom closet, put it on the living room table, and plugged it in.

"What's that?"

"You'll see." I got the cigar box with the cars in it off a shelf and put them on the track.

"Okay, what is it?"

"It's a slot-racing set. Got it this summer. Come on, give it a try."

She came over to the table. "What do I do?"

I told her how to work the control and gave her the Jaguar, taking the slower Corvette for myself. She ran slowly and cautiously at first, and I was able to lap her. She speeded up a bit then and went off at the next hairpin.

"I'm afraid this isn't my game."

"It does take a bit of practice."

"Well . . ."

I took the hint and put the cars back into their cigar box and turned off the transformer.

She sat back down on the sofa. I took a chair opposite her.

"Your suite is very nice."

"That's a hell of a way to put it. No, the suite's a bit better than what I had last year, at any rate."

"Oh, yes." She had finished her gimlet by now. "I guess I'd better be going. Studies and so forth."

"Sure." My own glass was still half full. "I'm glad you decided to come see the place."

"I really had wanted to come for some time."

"Well, thanks for coming."

"That's quite all right." She got up and went toward the door. I moved to get it for her. "And thank you for showing me around, Mr. Mercaptan."

I'd read enough Huxley to know about the hyperelegant litterateur with the couch he said was haunted by a poet. I laughed as well as I could. As she was just going out the door I said, "I assure you, there are no ghosts in *my* sofa."

12

Monday's *Daily Bulletin* published a long list of the new pairs of paramours who'd chosen to declare themselves on "their" day. Alphabetized by the last names of the ladies, the list recognized Joyce and Gary near its head. One could now, by local usage, refer to the Cleland-Forts.

They had to be careful to do their coeducational studying in public places, in order to keep their minds more or less on their work. Their good nights, though, were taking longer than ever, and took place inside her room or his.

Joyce finally legislated certain rules for them so that their arrangment would not damage their grades. They had to limit their time together during the week, and limit their activities within that time. They were to get as much work as possible out of the way in order to leave the weekends clear.

By contrast to his pre-paramour panic, Gary was completely relaxed. Every once in a while he thought of his old high-school buddies and wondered how many of them had this good a deal.

Gary came back to the office Monday afternoon, as requested.

"What's that funny pin?" I asked him, having noticed the salamander on his shirt.

"My paramour's favour."

"Oh. Congratulations."

"Thanks."

"It would appear that you got things settled all right."

"I think so."

"Good. Think you're up to making another decision now?"

"About working with you? There's no question about that."

"I take it you will."

"Of course."

"Congratulations again, then." There was a *scène-à-faire* handshake, and then I began briefing him in detail on everything I could think of connected with the magazine.

He listened attentively. When he thought he hadn't understood something right he asked about it. When I quizzed him on things I'd told him, he answered correctly.

"At the start you'll be doing everything our way," I said. "Soon enough, you'll be discovering your own ways of doing things. This is fine, but if they don't work it'll all be on your head."

He nodded.

"Okay, that's about it." I handed him a stack of manuscripts. "Go through these. I'll want recommendations on them by the end of the week. Give me your *reasons* whenever you can. Okay?"

"Okay."

"Go to it."

When he was back in the office as scheduled he seemed surprised at the third desk and chair just installed.

"Is this mine?"

"Of course. You didn't think we were going to have you sit on the floor, did you?"

"I hoped not."

"Okay. Move in anything you think you'll want to have here. Now then, your recommendations. I went through them last night."

"Uh-huh."

"Did you guess that some of those scripts weren't brand new submissions?"

He nodded.

"Well, I'm not sure that your recommendations were right. They all agreed pretty closely with what I did or would do with the particular scripts, but who knows whether that's 'right' or not."

He had looked disturbed, now looked relieved.

"Anyhow, I've made an appointment for you to tour the printshop Monday afternoon. You're to learn all you can about the various processes available, their capabilities, and their costs."

"Okay."

"Stop in here first and I'll make sure they've got some kind of guide set for you. For the rest of today, I'd like you to study as many back issues as possible, see what's already been used, and see how the magazine's developed. And take this home with you to study." I handed him a mimeographed copy of our financial breakdown. "Okay? Have fun."

Gary, Patty, and I were all busy at our respective desks when, for the first time that school year, the klaxons went off. Gary sat bolt upright.

"Is that—?" he shouted over the breakless raspy ooh-gahing.

"It is," I shouted back. "Come on."

We all sprang from our chairs. Patty grabbed her purse

and we left the office. I locked it and we headed for the Main Auditorium.

The halls were progressively more crowded as we got closer to it, everybody going in the same direction. At the doors there were floor supervisors with hand tallycounters, clicking off each student as he entered.

The auditorium was set up arena-style, with seats all around a central floor space, empty except for the administrator's desk and microphone and the Machine.

Gary, Patty and I took three seats together. Gary looked just a little green, and Patty was holding on to my arm.

The auditorium filled rapidly, despite the fact that students shuffled their feet as they came in. A man—a faculty member, chosen by lot—came in to stand at the administrator's desk. The floor supervisors who had been at the doors were now in a huddle, getting their total. Then they closed the doors and stood before them, and the klaxons stopped.

"A guillotine?" Gary said to me.

"Why not? It's quick, relatively merciful, and graphic. Keep quiet."

Patty already had her eyes shut. I watched Gary. His hands were tightly gripped on the edge of his seat.

The administrator blew once into the mike to make sure it was working, then began with a name. "Donald C. Pittenger."

One of the supervisors left his post to walk slowly down to the middle of the arena. All eyes that weren't shut followed him down.

"Donald C. Pittenger," the administrator said, "Your name has been selected at random from those of students whose grades have fallen below the minimum acceptable level. Do you understand?"

Pittenger nodded.

"Robert D. Thayer," the administrator said.

A student on the far side of the arena stood up, moved out to the aisle, and slowly walked down to the center. All unshut eyes now followed him.

"Robert D. Thayer," the administrator said to him, "Your name has been selected at random from those of students whose grades are within the highest range. Do you understand?"

Thayer nodded.

Under the close view of the administrator, Pittenger and Thayer took their places. Gary looked greener. The administrator nodded to Thayer and I shut my eyes. When I opened them Thayer still held the cord in his hand, looking as if he was going to be very ill, and Pittenger's head was in the basket.

I glanced at Gary. He looked more than a little sick. I supposed I should have warned him not to watch the whole thing, but guessed that he would have been unable not to. I had watched more of them myself than I'd wanted to.

The remaining supervisors now came down to the center. One helped Thayer make a rapid exit. The others made quick work of removing the parts of Pittenger's body. "Dismissed," the administrator finally said, and walked off.

"It's okay now, Patty," I said, and she opened her eyes.

"Thanks." She squeezed my arm once before releasing it.

"Gary, you okay?"

"I think so." His hands were still clenched to the edge of his seat. There were drops of sweat on his forehead.

Everyone was leaving now. "Come on," I said, "I'll give you a drink back at the office."

"I think I'd like one," Gary said.

Gary was to have met Joyce at one of the restaurants that evening. Now, early, he was waiting at her door for her to return from her last class of the day. He got the *Tumbrel* financial breakdown out of a pocket, unfolded it, and tried to read it as he waited. But he kept seeing Pittenger's head fall, again and again.

He glanced up from the sheets he was trying to read when he heard feet down the hall. It was Joyce, walking slowly. Her face was very pale. She didn't notice him immediately and he went down the hall to her.

"Gary." She almost fell onto his shoulder. "You saw it, didn't you?"

"I saw it."

"Wasn't it . . . ?"

"Come on, you've got to get dressed for dinner."

He helped her unlock her door, and then she wanted him to come into the room with her. He sat down on her sofa. Instead of starting to change, she sat down beside him.

"Gary, I fainted right there in the auditorium."

"Don't worry about it." He put his arm around her shoulders and they sat that way for several minutes. "Come on," he said finally, "we've got to go to dinner."

"Okay." She got up and changed clothes as he sat watching.

"We'll have a good meal in the quietest place we can find," he said. "And then afterwards we can get drunk if you want to."

"Tonight I think I might want to."

"Okay, and we'll forget all about this afternoon and we'll have a very good time."

"All right." She smiled for him as well as she could.

112

Dinner was as he'd promised her. He talked about the office and his assignments there, and she listened carefully. They sat there with drinks for quite a while after finishing the meal. Then by mutual consent they went up to his room, where there was still a little bit of the bourbon he'd bought weeks ago.

He was and was not surprised when, as soon as they were inside the room, she burst out crying. He sat with her on the sofa as they had that night in her room. She was talking chokingly, barely coherently. The drift was that she'd felt ashamed of herself, because she'd known about the Self-Discipline Plan before she'd come here, known about it and still been cocky enough to come.

He reassured her as well as he could, held her and rocked her, and got water for her. He didn't have to be told that this was no time for passion. Finally she went to sleep in his arms. He sat there with her, almost proud of himself, almost thanking her that she'd given him less time for reactions of his own to the execution.

He got her stretched out on the sofa and covered her up with an extra blanket. He arranged himself to sleep on the desk chair, arms folded and legs stretched out. Just before he drifted off, he remembered a time at least ten years before. He and his parents had been traveling with the family cat. He had sat in the back seat with the cat in its basket. It had been scared, and he had sung to it, crooning all the way in his boy-soprano.

13

"I'm afraid it really panicked her," Gary was telling me the following Tuesday afternoon at the office. I hadn't seen him since Friday.

"That's not too unusual, really," I said, "for the first time."

"Maybe so, but it still bothers me."

"I know. I'm afraid there's not much to do about it though."

Gary grunted.

The topic exhausted for the time being, I shifted over to quizzing Gary on his yesterday's tour of the printshop. He had notes to refer to, and I had no objection to these. He had his information.

"There's no point in hedging," I said. "If you can keep up your performance, you'll be editor of the frosh issue."

He smiled and nodded. "Thanks."

"Don't go thanking me. What it means is a lot of work for you and a vacation for me. But I think you'll manage."

"I hope so."

I nodded. "Oh, and there's another thing. They're not really connected. If it's all right with you, I'm going to propose you for membership in my club."

"I didn't know you were in a club."

"Sure. Tower. It's a pretty good group."

"Yeah, I'm told it's the best."

"Well . . . Anyhow, is it all right?"

"Sure. Thanks."

"Hell, it's nothing. Look, this is the deal. You'll be my guest tomorrow night. You'll be proposed at the business meeting."

"Uh-huh. What should I wear?"

"Safety suit'll be fine."

"You mean my uniform?"

"Yeah. White shirt, of course. Don't worry about it. It'll just be cocktails, dinner, the business meeting, and whatever we'll be having for entertainment—maybe just sit around and get crocked."

"Sounds good."

"I think you'll enjoy it."

"What does it cost, if I'm a member?"

"Per meeting, it's less than dinner for one at the Tower Room. You can swing it, can't you?"

"Yeah."

"Okay, then there shouldn't be any problem. I'll stop by for you at five-thirty tomorrow."

"Okay."

Then we got some magazine work done.

Gary was surprised and pleased by my invitation. He told Joyce only that he had some magazine work set for Wednesday night and wouldn't be able to study with her as usual. He hoped to be able to surprise her with news of his membership.

At five-thirty Wednesday, I knocked on his door.

"Come on in." He was just knotting his tie.

This was my first look at his room. I'd almost forgotten

how small the freshman cells were. I studied the Buffet, then glanced along his bookshelves.

He'd finished with the tie, shrugged his uniform blazer on, and ducked into the bathroom for his last mirror-check.

"I like the picture," I said.

"Thanks," he said. "I'm not quite sure why I picked it, but there it is."

Then he was all ready, and we left the room and started walking toward the club's suite.

"I see what you meant about the safety suit," he said.

I was wearing the uniform too. "All my purple dinner jackets are in the wash."

"I haven't made us late, have I?"

"No. Most of the guys get there any time between five-thirty and six. Compared with the average, we'll probably be a little early."

We got to the suite. The "Tower Club" plate was slipped into the holder on the door.

"Is this the club's permanent suite?"

"Not really," I said. "I mean, we always use this same one, but other times of the week it's used by non-social clubs and for meetings of faculty committees. None of the clubs keeps a suite of its own all the time—not when it can get one for its meetings for free."

We went inside. A few of my fellow members were already there, clustered around the bar, which Bert Lathrop, our seneschal, was tending. I began introducing Gary around.

"Bert, this is Gary Fort, the guest I told you about. Gary, this is Bert Lathrop, our current seneschal. He's the one we complain to about the menus."

"How do you do."

"How do you do."

117

They shook hands, and Bert asked Gary what he'd like to drink. Gary said bourbon and water, and then I continued the round of introductions.

"John Devereux, George Gibbs, Jim Klein, Frank Hoban . . ." Lots more how-do-you-do's and handshakes.

"I think you've seen Tom Curtis before."

"Of course. How do you do."

And so on. The room gradually filled with members and smoke. If Gary was helped by having a glass to clutch and sip at, he didn't show it.

"How'd that speech of mine sound for the convocation?" Curtis asked him.

"Sounded fine as far as I could tell."

"That's reassuring. Frankly, public speaking scares hell out of me. Especially in front of freshmen."

"I don't see why."

"Well, when they've just gotten here, they aren't used to the place yet—they aren't anesthetized yet."

"I think I see what you mean. But they're prepared to be shown how it works—I think they'd take your word for it."

Curtis nodded.

We continued around the room, flowing in the circular current from door to bar to appetizers to door. Gary seemed to be taking it all in stride, was able to embark easily on conversations with brand-new acquaintances—more easily than I had been when Heath had sponsored me.

I made a special point of introducing Gary to Mike Stokes, a sophomore who'd been proposed and accepted at the preceding week's meeting.

"It's really very simple," Stokes said. "They have the business meeting in the dining room after the table's been cleared, and they ask you to stay out here. Then they vote.

Sometimes, I'm told, they'll ask to see a guy here as a guest a second time, but not usually."

"Are you trying to scare me?" Gary asked, laughing.

"Hell, no," Stokes said.

"There shouldn't be any problem at all," I said.

"If you say so. The thing that really bothers me is that I'm the only one here with white tags."

"Big deal," I said.

At six-thirty we all moved to the dining room, sat down, and began eating without formalities. Gary did seem relieved at the simplicity of the meal—steak and potatoes, a salad, and pie—and kept up a quick conversation with Devereux, to his left, and Dennis Kirkby, to his right.

Then coffee and brandy, and those who wanted cigars took them from their pockets and smoked them. I stuck with my usual Luckies, and Gary, of course, didn't smoke at all.

Finally Lathrop rapped the side of his coffee cup with a spoon. "If nobody minds, I'll call the business meeting to order now. I'll have to ask our guest to step into the other room for the time being."

Gary quietly got up from his seat and went into the other room, closing the door behind him.

"Now then," Lathrop went on, "before we discuss the candidacy of Gary Fort, is there any other business?" There wasn't. "Okay. Duncan, would you care to say a few words?"

"Thanks, Bert." I stood up. "I met Gary through a submission he made to the *Tumbrel* a couple of weeks ago. I've been working with him since then. I believe all of you have met him by now, and I think you'll agree that he's all right." I sat down.

"Any other remarks?"

George Gibbs lifted a hand and stood up. "Duncan, are

you sure it isn't just that you want to propose the first freshman of the new year?"

"Somebody has to," I said. "Look, I'm not proposing the first freshman, or *a* freshman. I'm proposing Gary Fort."

"Okay." Gibbs laughed as he resumed his seat.

"Any other remarks?"

Curtis would have stood up to speak in Gary's favor, but it was not customary for anyone other than the sponsor to speak for a candidate unless he had been rejected and a new vote was desired.

"I'll call for a vote, then. All those in favor of the candidate."

Hands went up, some quickly, some slowly. Finally all were raised.

"Well, that's settled. Duncan, would you please bring the new member in?"

I nodded and went and got Gary. I indicated that he should approach the head of the table.

Everybody looked very solemn for a moment or two, then Lathrop put out his hand and said "Congratulations."

Gary looked startled for a second, then pumped Lathrop's arm enthusiastically. All the other members rose and formed a knot around him. I had trouble getting into the knot and was the last to offer my hand.

"Thanks, Duncan," he said.

"It's nothing." I noticed him massaging his right hand and wrist. "What's the matter?"

"Politician's arm." He smiled.

"Gary," Lathrop said, "catch me sometime later this evening for your membership card."

"Okay."

"And now, if you'll all retire to the other room," Lathrop said to the group, "we'll get on with the evening's entertainment."

After stops at the bar, all took seats in the other room. Devereux set up a screen and projector and showed some of his cinematic efforts, made that summer in the Chicago area. Most of them, and the best, were totally non-sequitur slapstick—chases and pie fights. Drinks were served between the films and after them. Jokes were traded, and almost everyone took a few minutes out to talk with Gary. As the evening was coming to an end, he looked a little tired but quite contented.

Finally it was over. Gary and I were headed to the elevators for our respective floors.

"Well?" I said.

"Well. Thanks again."

"Skip it."

"Say, Bert's been an executioner, hasn't he?"

"You noticed. . . . Most of them don't remind you of it that way."

"Yeah . . . By the way, your ribbons are a rather unusual combination, aren't they?"

"I suppose." I wore one black, one red, and four gray. "My first term I got off to a flying start, and then I sort of stumbled. You know, of course, that no matter how high your cumulative average is, if you go low enough in any term, they'll count you as being in low range."

"Yeah."

"Well, I had a term of chances. You can see I've been pretty safe since then."

Back at his room, he phoned Joyce with the good news. It was a little late and she sounded sleepy.

"I thought you'd want to hear about it. I didn't really

have magazine work tonight—I was accepted into Tower Club."

"That's wonderful."

"I'm not exactly displeased."

"Oh, Gary, I'm so proud of you!"

"I thought it'd make you happy."

"It does."

"Well, I guess we'd both better get some sleep. See you tomorrow."

"Tomorrow. G'night."

"G'night."

14

Friday night there was a play, a student production of Shaw. Gary hummed upbeat as he got dressed for it, wearing the uniform again. Just before going to pick up Joyce he saw himself in the mirror again, and struck his Ideal Student pose. He smiled. He felt absolutely set. He certainly ought to be, he thought—with a slot on the *Tumbrel* and a very good chance of the editorship of the freshman issue, with a very pretty paramour who was as good to have around in private as in public, and with membership in the top social club.

"You realize, of course," he said to his reflection, "that this is *it*."

With Joyce on his arm, he knew he made a good showing at the play. This was their first real date since his acceptance into Tower, and she was radiant. And his own manner, he was sure, could easily cause an upperclassman sizing him up to overlook the white tags on his uniform.

After the play and a couple of after-theater drinks, they went to his room, to make love in Buffet's empty plaza.

"Is everything all right?" he asked more or less rhetorically as they lay quiet in each other's arms.

"Couldn't be better," she said.

The next night there was a club party, definitely not stag. Gary was pleased with the reactions of his fellow members to Joyce, while their dates tended to be on much the same level of looks.

It was this evening that I finally met Joyce. There certainly was nothing wrong with her that I could see. I had taken the easy way out, was there with Patty, who didn't mind indulging me in this way. She was by now well known to all members of the club.

Gary dutifully made introductions around the four of us. Patty and Joyce got on well from the start, and soon were off in a cloud of female shoptalk. They spoke jokingly about disciplining Gary, Patty's charge while at the office, Joyce's at all other times.

While he and I were being completely ignored by our dates, I took the opportunity to fill him in on some further details of the club's operations: billing methods, frequency of parties, date-bureau service (not that he'd be needing it), election of our single officer, the seneschal.

The evening went on, with drinks, dancing to the small band, and much conversation. Gary was in his element and got progressively freer about letting alcohol into himself, as did Joyce. She clung tightly to him on the dance floor, earning them many amused smiles—not that they noticed.

In conversation, he was full of anecdotes. He made his home town of White Plains, New York, sound like a crazily interesting place, and his old buddies there seem like a bunch of happy idiots.

For myself, I didn't drink a lot—Patty and I watched out for each other. What I was wondering was why Gary was letting himself get so drunk. But when fragmentation time came, he and Joyce were still able to walk. I watched them going off down the hall.

The next morning he woke lying on his side, with Joyce's back pressed against his. He looked at the clock over on the desk. Ten forty-five. He turned, as easily as he could. Joyce's shoulders moved regularly. He could hear her breathing, unconscious sighs.

He furled back the sections of sheet and blanket that covered him and got up, trying to move the bed as little as possible. As it was, she stirred slightly but did not wake.

He stood there naked for a few moments, watching her as he rubbed his face with his hand. He wasn't hung over, but there was again the stupid feeling he always had on mornings after drinking too much. There was need of a shower and a shave, he knew, but there could be time for that later. What he wanted most right now was a cup of black coffee.

The clothes he had been wearing the night before were hung on the desk chair, intermingled with Joyce's. He extracted from the pile his shorts, socks, shirt, and trousers, and put them on. His belt buckle clanked annoyingly but didn't wake her.

He had to sit on the edge of the chair to tie his shoes—the greater part of the seat surface was taken up by her lingerie. He paused between right and left shoes to rub his eyes.

After standing up again, he ducked into the bathroom to check himself in the mirror. He'd get by, at least to go for coffee. Half the people who got up on Sunday mornings looked raunchier than he did.

From his desk top he grabbed a pencil and the nearest paper, an old envelope. He wrote "Out for coffee. Back soon" on it and balanced it on top of the clothing on the chair, so that she would see it if she woke before he returned. After pocketing his wallet and key, he moved slowly and carefully on the door knob, making minimum noise. Outside, he closed the door the same way. He paused for a moment, then locked it with his key.

In the elevator down, his slow memory dredged up some very hazy scenes from the preceding night. Oh God, he couldn't remember what had happened after that conversation with Devereux. Maybe Duncan could.

On arriving at the first floor, he went to the nearest phone cubby.

"Hello."

"Hello, Duncan?"

"Who else?"

"I didn't wake you, did I?"

"No, I've been up for about an hour. What is it?"

"Last night. I'm afraid I can't remember too much of it."

"Neither, I should think, can a lot of others. What about it?"

"Well, I was wondering if anything—untoward happened?"

"Nothing that I can recall."

"Uh-huh."

"If anything had happened, somebody else besides you would have called me by now."

"I suppose . . . I know Joyce was acting a little too affectionate, maybe."

"Big deal. Look, nobody dislikes you or her. Forget it."

"Okay. I guess it's all right, then."

"Sure it is. Good God, stop worrying. You're a member and she's your paramour."

"True."

"Are you hung?"

"No. I just feel like somebody's lopped about forty points off my IQ."

"You had any breakfast yet?"

"No. I was just going for coffee."

"Well, go get some and take it easy. A little caffeine'll improve your whole outlook."

"Okay. Thanks."

"It's nothing. Hope you get to feeling smarter. And don't forget to come to the office tomorrow afternoon."

"Okay. See you tomorrow."

"See you."

Gary went to the snack bar and got two cups of coffee to go. He thought of getting something to eat, but didn't feel really hungry yet.

On the way back to the elevators he passed a cigarette machine and for some reason paused at it. Setting his coffee down on its top, he dug into his trouser pocket, found he had the correct change, and put it into the machine. Something fairly weak, he figured, to start on. He pushed the button for Kents.

There was something very neat, very smooth, very compact about the cellophane-wrapped packet that came out, recalling junior high experiments with tobacco, inconclusive ones. There was still something magical about an unopened pack of cigarettes. He put the pack into his shirt pocket and the matches that came with it into a trouser pocket.

He was very quiet about unlocking and opening the door, despite a juggling act with the coffee cups. Joyce was still asleep. He set one of the cups on the shelf above her head, then closed the door very quietly. He put the other cup down on his desk, then crumpled his note and tossed it into the wastebasket by the desk, and moved all the clothing from the chair to the lowboy so that he could sit down a bit more comfortably.

He removed the lid from his coffee cup, which was made of some kind of foamed plastic. He had a thorough acquaintance with coffee in cardboard cups, and was perverse enough to prefer it that way. He took a sip from the plastic cup. Still too hot.

Now he took a virgin ashtray from a desk drawer and set it before him. The pack of cigarettes seemed such a complete, finished product that he hesitated before opening it. He tapped out a cigarette, aware of his clumsiness in executing the movement, and put it between his lips. He got the book of matches out of the trouser pocket, opened it, tore one out, closed the cover of the book, struck the match, and held it close to the end of the cigarette. There were tiny rustlings as the cigarette lit, nothing in comparison with the scruff and blowing noise of the match-lighting. The first puff of smoke, which got only as far as his mouth, didn't taste like much.

He remembered how you could blow smoke out through your nose without inhaling it. But wasn't this sort of half inhaling, and maybe if he practiced it . . . He practiced, with variations, and soon found that he actually was taking small amounts of smoke into his lungs. Then he remembered instructions from high school friends, about how you took a puff of smoke into your mouth, then took some air in with it as you inhaled. He tried that too.

By the time he was on his fourth Kent, he was taking fairly deep drags. He was more or less alternating these with sips of his coffee, which by now was at a drinkable temperature.

He heard Joyce stirring with the bedclothes and turned to look at her.

She turned over and now faced in his direction. Her eyes were half open.

"Good morning."

"G'morning," she said. "You're smoking."

"Uh-huh. Drink your coffee."

15

Gary didn't forget to show up at the office. I came in after he did. Patty was sitting there trying not to laugh, watching him smoke a cigarette.

After offering greetings to the two of them, I told Gary he was doing it all wrong.

"Well, I am a beginner, after all."

"Okay," I said. "Smoking lesson number one, right now."

Patty chuckled and turned to address the paperwork on her desk.

"First off, don't wrap your lips around the damned thing. The idea is to hold it as lightly as possible and still get smoke intake."

He tried it.

"Okay, and don't take such deep breaths—are you trying to smoke or hyperventilate?"

"Smoke."

"All right, then. Smoking's supposed to be a relaxing thing. So act relaxed."

He made a noticeable effort to do so, with some success.

"Couple more things. You don't have to keep the cigarette in your hand the whole time it's going. The ashtray isn't just for putting them out in and holding butts."

He obediently set his cigarette down in the ashtray, then picked it up again, took a puff, held the cigarette out, and stared at it as he exhaled.

"That's the other thing. The only people who look lovingly at their cigarettes are the people in cigarette commercials on TV. I can see where you've gotten your examples."

"Well . . ."

"Well . . . You're supposed to take your smoke for granted. It's not an object of attention, except when you're lighting it or putting it out."

"Okay." Staring fixedly at the far wall, he took another puff.

"What are you smoking?" Then I noticed the pack on the desk. "Gawd, those things! Well, I guess they're all right for a start. We'll graduate you to cigarettes soon enough. If you really get your lessons down, I'll let you have a couple of Sobranies."

"Sobranies?"

"Sobranies—what this country needs is a good nickel cigarette. No, I think the only cigarettes I ever really enjoyed were my first Sobranies."

"Just your first ones?"

"Yeah. You can get used to anything."

"What do you usually smoke?—Luckies, isn't it?"

"Uh-huh."

"How come?"

"Superstition, I guess. . . . Say, when did this business start?"

"You mean the smoking?"

"Yeah. When?"

"Yesterday morning, just a little while after I talked to you."

"Oh, great. Now it's on my head."

He gave me a sour look for that.

"How did it start?"

"I don't know. I just thought I'd teach myself to smoke."

"There had to be a reason."

"I don't know. . . . Since yesterday I've felt kind of grouchy. I don't know why."

"Why should you?"

"I shouldn't. My courses are going fine, I like the work here, Joyce is great, and so is the club."

I couldn't help a small laugh. "You thought it'd take so little to satisfy you?"

Gary looked up suddenly. "What?"

"You heard me."

"So what should it take?" he asked slowly.

That I couldn't answer. "If you don't know, no one does."

Saturday was Homecoming. Gary was in his room getting ready for the game when there was a knock on his door.

"Come in." Gary thought it would be Pryor, the floor supervisor, bearing toilet paper.

It wasn't Pryor. It was a man in his early or middle twenties, wearing an MU uniform with gold-colored shoulder tags.

"I hope you don't mind me stopping in. My name's Craig Downs."

"Gary Fort."

They shook hands.

"You see, I had this room when I was a freshman. That was . . . six years ago."

"Uh-huh."

"Still looks about the same. . . . I see the desk's been changed, though."

"Have a seat."

"Thanks." Downs sat on the sofa. "Lots of memories here, in such a small space."

"I think I know what you mean." Gary sat down in the desk chair and took his pack—Marlboros, now—from his pocket. "Cigarette?"

"Got my own, thanks." Downs produced a pack of Pall Malls, gave Gary and himself lights.

"Thanks. Is . . . this your first time back?"

"No, I always make it for Homecoming. First time in years that I've seen this room, though."

"I hope you approve of the way I'm keeping it."

"Sure. Looks just about the same as ever. I had a different picture on the wall, though. I forget exactly what it was—something with nymphs and satyrs, I think."

"You're two years out, aren't you?"

"That's right. Going for my doctorate at Harvard now, in math."

Gary nodded. "How'd you like it here?"

"Pretty well. I was high mid-range most of the time, went into the black once or twice. Never was an axeman—which was just as well as far as I was concerned."

"I kind of take it you took advantage of the facilities while you were here."

"Oh yeah. Club and all that, spent lots of time in the bars."

"Which club?"

"Compass. We had some good times."

"Two of the guys across the hall—Frazier and Liebman—joined Compass just this week."

Downs nodded. "You in one too?"

"Tower."

Downs nodded again. "Good bunch."

"I think I agree. I only joined this week myself."

Downs smiled. "Busy week."

"Yeah." Gary passed the ashtray.

"Ah . . . it's good to get back to the old place. Nothing else is quite like it."

"I shouldn't think so."

"No . . . I'll tell you, the time you spend here can be the best or the worst of your life. I've seen guys do it both ways. But your chances—pardon the expression—your chances here are so great. You've just got to take advantage of them."

"If you had it to do over again, would you still come here?"

"Well . . . that's sort of another question."

PART TWO

16

A night late in November, during what would have been
Thanksgiving vacation, had the University given us a vacation for Thanksgiving. I'd spent the evening alone in my
suite, working on my private enterprise, "Who Is Duncan
Chase?" It had been transcription of handwritten notes to
start with, and then a little new material. There had been
many long pauses for cigarettes, sips of beer, and favorite
passages in the records I was playing. Trying to puzzle out
myself and people I'd known, I hadn't felt lonely.

I'd packed away my typewriter and papers and was
thinking about turning in, when somebody came to the
door.

"Gary. Come on in."

"Thanks. I know it's late, but I was hoping you'd still
be up."

"Sure. Can I get you a beer?"

"Thanks."

I got him one and another for myself. We popped tops
and sat down.

"What have you been doing tonight?" he asked.

"Not a hell of a lot. Working a little on that thing I told
you about."

"You'll have to show it to me sometime."

"Well . . ."

"I know. Just kidding." He addressed himself to a good slug of beer.

"What's up with you?" I asked after a slug for myself.

"Well . . ." He dug into a jacket pocket, then was holding up something small between thumb and forefinger. "This."

"Can't see it from here."

He tossed it to me. It was a tie-tack, made from a small piece of polished stone. "Haven't I seen Joyce wearing this?"

"It's the favour I gave her. Was."

"What happened?"

He spread his hands, "I got it back tonight." He took another slug from his beer can.

"Her idea or yours?"

"Mine—I don't really know why."

I lit myself a cigarette. As if I'd reminded him, he got out a pack of Camels—it looked as if he'd be sticking with that brand—and lit one.

"God," he said, "was it bad."

"I take it she didn't much care for the idea."

"Hell, no."

"What'd you give her as a reason?"

"I don't think I gave her any reason. I don't know."

I took a good swallow of beer. "You don't seem too exhilarated with your freedom. Wasn't it what you wanted?"

"I don't know." He was shaking his head, then took more beer.

I grunted. "Well, I guess that's that."

"I'm afraid it is."

We sat for a while, quietly smoking our cigarettes and working on our cans of beer.

Finally I grunted again. "Something I want you to

hear." I got up and put on a jazz album I'd bought that day.

As the music played he sat staring, as if concentrating on it.

"There," I said when the trumpet solo on the first band started.

He kept staring, nodding occasionally.

After the side had ended I got us refills on the beers. Then we heard the other side. After that I got out the slot-racers and put something less attention-demanding on the turntable. We ran numberless races and drank countless beers. Gary finished his pack of cigarettes and bummed a couple of my Luckies. I got to yawning, and he finally did too.

"God, it's late," he said. "I'd better get going. Got to get some sleep sometime."

"Me too." We moved to the door.

"Thanks," he said on his way out.

I held up a hand. "It's nothing. See you at the office Monday." After he'd left, I picked up the beer cans, emptied the ashtrays, and put away the slot-racers.

I saw Gary regularly at the office and at club meetings. But otherwise he was practically invisible. He didn't go to any of the club parties and he took all his meals but Wednesday-night dinner by himself. At the office he was quiet and businesslike, keeping his head bent over his desk. He was courteous when spoken to but rarely initiated nonessential conversation. His own writing had dwindled away—he was doing only editorial work now. At club meetings he drank his full share, but never did seem to loosen up. The other members began wondering and asked me what was wrong with him. I could only relate to them the bare outlines of the story I knew. He must have been smoking two packs of Camels a day.

His life had become a curious parody of my own. He worked hard on his studies and the magazine, stayed in his room most of the time, went almost nowhere, and saw almost no one. Once Patty "let" him take her to dinner—his relationship with her was by now about the same as mine—and she was able to confirm my impressions. She learned, in fact, that he had taken as his model what he knew of the way I was living.

I'd remind him of every party, suggest that he let the club get him a date. He'd always demur. I'd remind him even more vehemently of the no-date parties, the ones only paramours could attend as couples—in practice, pick-up parties—that always had good supplies of unattached girls. He'd still demur.

I began to get a bit angry with him—for turning his satiric talents on my precious way of life.

One evening I'd had enough of my suite and went out to one of the bars for my beers. There was Gary at one of the back tables. I got myself a draft and went to join him.

"Evening," I said.

"Hi, Duncan. Have a seat."

"Thanks. I wasn't expecting to see you here."

"Well, I have to get out of the room every so often."

"I know what you mean."

We finished our existing rounds, then split a pitcher.

"What have you been doing with yourself?" I asked. "Nobody seems to see much of you."

"I've been trying to keep busy. Got to keep the studies up."

"You didn't seem to be having any trouble keeping them up before."

"Well . . ."

I nodded and we went back to silent drinking. Then I tried to guess his state of mind. "Did I ever tell you I had a paramour once?"

"No."

"Last year. Late fall until the end of spring. It was great."

"What happened?"

"It ended."

He paused for reflection and a sip of beer before asking, "How come?"

"I'm not sure I know, even now. Suddenly it was all over—as if it were by mutual consent. But neither of us ever said anything. I don't know."

He nodded, then sipped from his glass again. "What was she like?"

"Great," I said, "that's all."

He smiled, then lit a cigarette.

17

I got fed up. The last Friday before exams, toward the middle of December, I was pounding on Gary's door.

"Hi, Duncan. What is it?"

"As you know, the club is giving its last party of the term tonight. You're going to it."

"You know I can't go. I haven't got a date."

"Yes you do. Her name is Barbara Tillman. All you have to do is call her."

He gave me one of the sourest looks I'd ever seen. "I've never even met her."

"Neither have I. But I got her name from lists kept by our trusty seneschal. I understand she's planning on studying tonight, but you should be able to persuade her to come out for a term-end blowout."

"Hell, let her study. I don't want to be responsible for making some girl I've never met take the chance."

"If she winds up taking the chance because of you, you'll know her by then."

He still was looking sour at me. "Duncan, I really wasn't planning on going anywhere tonight."

"What *were* you going to do tonight?"

He pulled a paperback edition of *You Can't Go Home Again* off his bookshelf. "Read this."

"Great. Plenty of time for that later."

"I don't suppose you have a date for tonight."

"As a matter of fact, I do."

"Patty?"

"No, she got invited out from under me to the Compass blowout. No, my date is one Gwen Morris."

"Never heard of her."

"Neither had I until I met her in a bar last night. When was the last time you had a date?"

"I don't know."

"Then you really *are* in bad shape. Look, just call this Tillman girl. Make an honest effort, and if she still doesn't want to go after hearing your melodious tones, we'll forget the whole thing. Okay?"

He snarled but moved to the phone. "What's the number?"

I dug the slip of paper with the number on it out of my pocket, then sat down on the sofa and lit a cigarette.

"Hello, Miss Barbara Tillman? . . . My name is Gary Fort. I'm doing a survey on how many girls are academically confident enough to go to parties the last Friday night before term finals. . . . That's right. Tower Club . . . They said I'd call—" he shot me a very annoyed look— "Well, gee, I'm just an average guy—green hair, webbed feet, five eyes. . . . You do? Then we've got an even dozen between us. What do you say? . . . Yes, but think of all the time you'll still have to study. Forty-eight hours, maybe. . . . You will? . . . Good. Just a second." He covered the mouthpiece. "Duncan, what time's the party start?"

"Eight-thirty."

"Party starts at eight-thirty. So I'll be by for you, about, oh, eight twenty-three. Okay? . . . Fine. See you then . . . So long." He hung up the receiver.

"Very well done."

"She'll probably be a pig."

"You know damn well the club wouldn't fix you up with a pig. I'm sure she's positively lovely."

"And nine feet tall."

"That I wouldn't know about. Read your Wolfe real fast and get dressed. I'll be back around eight-fifteen to check up on you."

"You really trust me, don't you?"

"Sure, about as far as I can toss the Tower. I'll see you later."

"Yeah." At least he was smiling.

"What's he doing?" Gwen asked me. She, Gary, and I were standing in the hall in front of Barbara Tillman's door. Gary was staring at his watch.

"Waiting for the Right Moment," I said, and explained.

At eight twenty-three, Gary knocked on the door. It opened, and Barbara Tillman appeared unto us.

"Good evening." Gary didn't work very hard at concealing his not unhappy surprise.

Neither did she. "Good evening."

"All ready to go?"

"Uh-huh." She locked her door, then chucked the key into her small purse and the four of us, after a round of introductions, in which Miss Tillman asked to be called Barb, were off.

"Didn't you forget something?" Gary asked.

"Oh, that's right," Barb said. "I left five of my eyes behind."

"Well, that's all right. I forgot my other three."

She clicked her tongue at him and shook her head. "No organization."

We got to the party and all worked very hard at Having

a Good Time on our Last Chance Before Exams. Gwen and I got along acceptably, if not famously. Gary seemed to be having fun despite himself, dancing just about as often as the band played, drinking much and pretty well, talking almost continuously with Barb.

They had spates of conventional conversation during the evening: home towns, majors, reactions to freshman rooms. Barb was also a freshman, from a suburb of Cleveland, majoring in English, and had been lucky enough to get a room with a window.

"Why did you come to MU?" he asked her.

"I wanted the best party school I could get. How about you?"

"The only other application I made was rejected." This was accurate enough, but only half truth. His one other application, to his father's old school, had been made halfheartedly and undoubtedly had read that way. Somehow, after hearing her reason, he didn't want to mention the enthusiasm for MU that had colored most of his senior year in high school, his feelings then of getting something better, academically as well as in other ways, than any of his classmates were getting in their college choices. And the Self-Discipline Plan—then, half the time he hadn't believed in it, the other half it had seemed something almost romantic.

"Congratulate me," I said.

"What for?" Gwen asked.

"For that." I used my chin to point to Gary and Barb, dancing again. "This is the first date he's had since he broke up with his paramour. That was weeks ago."

"Congratulations."

"Thank you."

"Looks like he's trying to make up for lost time."

"He'll be all right. Cigarette?"

146

Now Gary and Barb stood at the bar while Gwen and I were dancing.

"Got a great idea," Gary said.

"What?"

"Let's get out of here."

"But this is your party."

"My club's party—great bunch of guys. No, we've made our appearance. Now we can go someplace else."

"Where, for instance?"

He spread his hands slowly. "My room, maybe?"

"What's there?"

"Privacy."

"What do we need privacy for?"

"To count our eyes."

She laughed. "I think we can do that here." She pointed her index finger at his face. "One. Two."

He made the same motions. "Three. Four. Great. Now I'll have to think of some other excuse."

"Let me know when you do."

"I will."

"Fine. Let's have another drink."

More or less by general agreement, the party was dissolving. The four of us who had arrived together stood waiting for elevators, about to split up into couples.

"God, it's late," I was saying. "For so close to finals, anyway."

"Very true," Gary said. Then an elevator going in his direction arrived. He and Barb stepped into it, and quick good nights were offered back and forth. "Hey, Duncan," he said just as the door was about to close, "Thanks."

"S'okay." I waved, and then the door was shut.

Gary and Barb got off the elevator at her floor. He was singing, not too loudly, a song that was currently popular. She joined in. He had to solo again as she concentrated on getting her key out of her purse and opening her door.

"You mean you aren't going to ask me in—to see your window?"

"Not tonight, really."

He spread his hands, then gathered her into his arms and kissed her. She didn't seem to mind.

"I really had a very good time."

"So'd I. Thanks."

"G'night, Gary."

"G'night." He whistled his way back to the elevators.

The next day, Gary's record player came. He'd written his parents before, asking them to send it. Now, just before end of term, it was here, along with a number of his records. It arrived in the morning; that afternoon he returned to the University Package Store for another bottle of bourbon. Most of the rest of the afternoon was devoted to polishing off some class assignments, with an occasional smile directed to the new bottle over on the shelf. At five he hit the phone.

"Hello, Barb? Gary Fort."

"Hi, Gary. How are you?"

"Okay. You?"

"Okay."

"That's good. Say, I hope I didn't annoy you last night."

She laughed softly. "Of course not."

"That's good. Look, I was wondering if you'd like to have dinner with me tonight?"

"I'm afraid I've already got a date for dinner tonight."

"Couldn't you get out of it? I really would like to see you again tonight."

"I suppose I could try."

"Would you? This time of the term, it should be easy enough to beg off."

"I'll see what I can do. I'll have to call you back."

"Right." He gave her his number.

"Okay. I'll call you back just as soon as I know."

"Okay. Thanks."

"That's all right. 'Bye for now."

"So long." Gary replaced the receiver, moved to sit on his sofa, and read for twenty minutes in a book he pulled at random from his shelves. Then his telephone rang.

"Barb?"

"Uh-huh."

"What's the word?"

"The word's okay. What time are you coming by?"

"Six-thirty all right?"

"Fine."

"Good. What did you tell him?"

"Said I had a headache and I thought I'd better try to study tonight if I could."

"Gave it to him with both barrels. Very good."

"Where are we going?"

"A wonderful little restaurant. The food is excellent, but the place isn't brassy like the Tower Room."

"Sounds good. I'd better start getting ready."

"Me too. See you at six-thirty."

"See you then."

After getting off the phone, Gary took a quick shower and shave and got into his uniform. Finding himself all ready and running ahead of schedule, he opened the bottle and poured himself a little one. He took all the time he needed to over it, then started for Barb's room.

They went to the little restaurant Frazier had discovered so long before, where Gary and Joyce had taken so many meals together.

"Good?" he asked after the table had been cleared preparatory to dessert.

"Very."

"That's good. I'd hoped you'd like it."

"This place is quite pleasant."

"I agree."

Dessert came and was finished, and they were sitting over coffees.

"Cigarette?" Gary said.

"Thanks, but I'll stick to my own." She drew a pack of a filtered brand from her purse. He got out matches and lit their cigarettes.

"Where do we go from here?" she asked.

"Well, now, weren't you saying to some guy, just a little earlier this evening, that you really *had* to study tonight?"

She frowned.

"Actually," Gary said, "I was thinking . . . I got this Care package from home today."

"Care package?"

"My folks finally sent me my record player."

"Oh."

"Anyhow, they sent me some of my records along with it, so I was thinking, if you dared, maybe we could listen to a few of them. We could have a couple of drinks, too."

"This sounds just like what you were trying to talk me into last night."

"Not at all. I didn't have the record player then."

"I see. Well, you do look like a wholesome lad . . ."

"Don't I, though."

". . . so I guess it should be all right."

"Certainly. As Dr. Clark was saying just the other day:

'Wholesome lad, Gary Fort. No one else I'd rather see escorting my daughter or any other young girl.' "

"He doesn't have a daughter, does he?"

"That's beside the point. Shall we?"

"Of course."

They stubbed out their cigarettes and left the restaurant.

"The room's Standard Freshman Gothic, I'm afraid," Gary said as he unlocked his door.

"That's all right."

They went inside. "The Winter Palace," Gary said.

"Charming," said Barb.

They sat on the sofa with their drinks, with the record player going—a decent stereo machine he'd gotten at Lafayette in Scarsdale. They paid close attention to the various bits of music. Barb seemed to approve of his taste. Right now, his "Threepenny Opera" album was on, and he was consciously having to keep himself from humming along, especially on bands like the "Army Song."

She got out another of her cigarettes. He brought out his matches again and cursed them cheerfully as he was unable to get a light on the third stroke.

"Why don't you get yourself a lighter?" she asked.

"Because I'd be sure to lose it within a week."

She got her lighter—one of the attractive push-button ones that are no good in the slightest breeze—out of her purse and handed it to him.

"Thanks." He lit her cigarette, quickly got out and lit one of his Camels. "Can I get you another drink?" Both their glasses had sat empty for several minutes now.

"I really don't think so."

"As you wish." With his cigarette firmly planted in his mouth, he got up and mixed himself another. He brought back his full glass and set it down beside her empty one.

Almost simultaneously, they put their cigarettes down in the ashtray.

"Barb . . ."

Then he was kissing her again. It was all easy enough.

It was when his hand started moving up her thigh that she objected, with a very businesslike "uh-uh."

"What's the matter?"

"I just said uh-uh. No go."

"Why not? You don't like it?"

"That's not the point. . . . Gary, I'm not going to throw 'morality' at you. It's just that I draw the line at certain things until there are assurances."

"What kind of assurances do you need to let me put my hand on your thigh?"

"Oh, Gary . . . We just met last night, after all."

"Yeah, I know, I know."

"It's not that I don't like you."

"That's something."

"Gary, I'd be happy enough to let you go all the way, if . . ."

"If what?"

". . . If we were to trade favours."

He laughed, a short bark. "I believe you've misunderstood the whole point of the paramour system."

"Well . . ." She started rebuttoning her blouse.

"Really. Here, over the years, this fine, noble tradition has grown up, of true love and youthful lust. MU students hopelessly in rut find themselves staring at each other across the bedsheets the next morning and wondering how they can dignify what they've done. Enter the paramour system, which joyfully grants complete social acceptability —on the local level, at least—to whatever kind of teamwork they may care to indulge in. *This*, my dear, is the paramour system—and you're making a mockery of it."

"I really think . . ." By now she was picking up her purse and standing up.

"Barb honey, I suppose someday some guy'll be completely charmed by your refreshing candor. But I'm not him. You aren't leaving, are you?"

"Good night, Gary." She closed the door hard after her.

"Good night." He was laughing—a bit hollowly, he knew—as he picked up his glass again.

So much for Barb Tillman.

18

Final examinations for the term were Monday through Friday of the following week. He caught the last bus of the day out of the valley, and then got the train. He'd wondered if he might run into Joyce in transit. They had long since changed their seats in their common class, and hadn't passed more than a word since the night in November when he got his favour back, except for an exchange of "good lucks" just before their History of Film final. He didn't see her on the bus or the train. She'd apparently finished up and left already. It was just as well as far as he was concerned.

All his fellow passengers on the bus were MU students and so were many on the train. He, like almost everyone else, was tired but relieved; a few seemed nervous about the outcome of exams. The ride was not unpleasant—he'd brought along the remainder of his bottle of bourbon and many of the others had also brought refreshments. The breaking-up of the group at Grand Central was the end of a party.

Back in White Plains, he found himself in the middle of another party. The invitation had been waiting for him when he'd gotten home—it was a reunion of sorts, hosted by one of his high-school classmates.

"So how's Modern life?" Forby was asking him.

"Not too bad," Gary said. "Single room and a private john. More bars than you can shake a stick at. Sometimes you have to share your room, though."

"Huh?"

"The ladies—they have this funny thing about staying by themselves all night in their own rooms."

"Oh." Forby laughed. "Is that the Old School Tie you're wearing?"

"Uh-huh. In fact, this is the uniform." Gary was wearing his full MU uniform, less shoulder tags. "See?" He showed Forby the seal on the buttons of his blazer.

"Yes. Say, Gary, is Modern really as good academically as everybody says it is?"

"As far as I can tell. I haven't had any of the special things yet—you know, the underclassmen seminars, tutorials, and so forth—but the faculty seems to be really good. Next term I'm going to be in one of the special deals—Basic Editorial Workshop, sort of a round table for underlings on the publications. I'm on the humor-lit magazine, the *Tumbrel*."

"What's it got a name like that for?"

"I don't know. Tradition or something."

Forby nodded, then was collared by someone else. Gary moved to refill his glass. Although he'd had highest expectations for this party, some unconscious premonition had made sure that he brought along a bottle. There was no problem with driving, as he'd ridden with Martelli, this year a senior at White Plains High.

"Hi, Gary."

"Hi, Kay. How are you?"

"Okay." Three months in Poughkeepsie didn't seem to have done her any harm. "You?"

"As usual." He spread his hands.

"How do you like Modern?"

"Pretty well. How's Vassar?"

"It's still there. But you pretty much have to like Modern, don't you? That's the one you can't transfer out of."

"That's right. But I think I'll be able to stick it out."

"That's good. When'd you get off?"

"Friday. Finished up finals and started traveling."

"That's kind of late, isn't it?"

"Yeah, and we didn't get Thanksgiving off."

She frowned. "I guess you'd really better like the place."

"Yeah." He smiled. "But it's really not bad. I've got a private room, a little stock of booze, and I'm on the magazine and in one of the social clubs."

"Clubs?"

"Uh-huh. No fraternities, so we've got these clubs. Mine's Tower. They're all strictly local, of course."

"Does your club have a house?"

"We take a suite in the Tower for our meetings and parties. You know the whole University's in one building."

She nodded. "That should be convenient in cold weather."

"Yeah. I could have gone all term without going outside —except for football games, of course."

"Of course."

"Really, everything you need is inside, even the bars."

"Very good."

"It works out." He brought out his cigarettes and lit one.

"And you've started smoking."

"Well, yes. It was kind of funny. One morning I just bought myself a pack of cigarettes and decided I'd teach myself to inhale."

"At least you do it well."

"Don't tell anyone, but I took lessons."

"I see. Don't worry, I won't tell."

"Thanks."

And then after a while Kay was gone again, and Gary was left by himself with his drink and cigarette.

He continued through the evening's rounds of talking, smoking, and drinking. He was glad to be seeing some of these people again. Harmon, Wilson, Phyllis, Janet. But he gradually realized that, quite simply, this crowd wasn't his crowd any more. He got quietly tight and talked more with Martelli than anyone else—Martelli had applied to MU.

"You know, when I had my interview, they told me about this Self-Discipline Plan. Is it true?"

"It's true."

"I still can't quite believe it."

"You'd better. Believe it, and then see if you still want to go to MU. If you do, good enough."

"What's it really like there?"

"Apart from the Self-Discipline Plan, it's great. It's just great—your own room with your own john, bars, stores, even night clubs—you've got to go to the Tower Room once, at least."

"What about social life?"

"Well, a club helps, but even without one it's pretty good. There's a mixer every Friday night, and you can meet girls in the bars, too. And there're no restrictions on visiting-hours or anything like that."

"Nobody minds if you have a girl in your room?"

"Hell, no—so long as the girl doesn't mind."

"Is there a lot of going steady?"

"Yes, but we don't call it that. If a guy and a girl want to . . . officialize themselves, each gives the other a 'favour,' and from then on they're paramours—a publicly accepted couple—until they take their favours back."

"Sounds okay. I just still can't believe that about the Self-Discipline Plan. Do they really . . . ?"

Gary nodded. "That's right. That's the one thing you've got to take seriously. Because once you're in, the only way you can get out is to either graduate or get the ax."

"God! But still . . ."

"Yeah," Gary said. "But still, it seems like it's worth the risk."

"Have you gotten any grades yet?"

"Not yet. They'll be mailing them home soon. I went into my finals with A's, but I can't be sure."

"Are you worried at all?"

"Sure. You never can know until you get the final grades."

"Yeah."

"Does it seem disenchanting to you?"

"No, not really."

"Duncan?"

"Yeah. Gary?"

"Yeah. How are you?"

"More or less surviving." I was experiencing again that sense of discovery you have when someone you know from school calls you at home. "What's up?"

"Nothing much. My grades came today."

"How were they?"

"A's."

"Nice going, axeman."

"Cut it out. Did you get yours?"

"Uh-huh. Few B's in there. One more gray ribbon."

"Good."

"I suppose . . . When'd you get in?"

"Early Saturday. I had a final in the last slot on Friday."

"Well, I've been down since Thursday night and there's still nothing much going on."

"I know. How about some pubbing tonight?"

"Sure. Anyplace in particular?"

"I could show you the hot spots of White Plains."

"Sounds okay. Shall I pick you up at your place?"

"Fine. About eight?"

"Eight's fine. How do I get there?"

He gave me the directions to his house.

"Okay," I said. "I should make it, with luck. See you at eight."

"Right. So long."

"So long."

So I got a car from the folks and drove down the Saw Mill River Parkway to White Plains. I kept the heater on and the radio tuned to WMCA. There was no snow on the ground. Christmas was coming up within the week—looked like it'd be another green one.

Gary must have been waiting just inside his front door, because he came out as I pulled into the driveway. He popped into the car, we swapped greetings, and then I backed out again.

Downtown White Plains was something of a mess. Almost all the stores were open for late shopping, and people were everywhere. But I had a certain familiarity with the section from shopping there, and there were Christmas-tree effects on the lampposts.

We headed for a fairly quiet tavern on Post Road, not the noisier one that was the big pickup bar in town. I got a parking space somehow and we went inside. We got our first drafts of Bud, Gary covering this round, and took a table at the back.

"Went to a party last night," he said. "The old high-school crowd."

160

"How was it?"

"Bad. It wasn't at all what I was expecting. It seems like there's no cohesiveness to the group any more. You know?"

"I know."

He nodded. "I should have known."

"So you're a potential executioner now," I went on. "Congratulations."

"Thanks. I hope it doesn't come to that."

"I wouldn't worry about it."

"Okay."

We proceeded to get good and tight, swapping rounds of the good old Budweiser, talking about the magazine—which would require a great flurry of work as soon as we got back—about our finals, trips home, and anything else that came to mind.

"I wonder if I could find Joyce's number," Gary said. "Can't be too many Clelands in Mamaroneck."

"You really want to see her?"

"I'd like to talk to her again at least. She'd probably hang up on me. Wouldn't blame her."

"Neither would I, frankly."

A few more rounds and we were singing the MU fight song, the alma mater, and obscene variations of them perpetuated by Tower Club. The bartender gave us indulgent smiles—it was a slow night, all the kids up at the pickup joint, all the older people doing their shopping.

We moved to the bar so that we could watch TV—one medium that is somehow improved by an alcoholic stupor. We sat through the news and all of the Late Show, then decided to skip the Late Late Show and headed out.

"Hey!" I said, and Gary echoed.

There was a light powdering of snow on the ground and more of it being shaken down gently from the sky.

"This is great!" Gary said.

"Except that I've got to drive home in it." We went to the car and had to wipe a light coating of snow off the windows before starting.

"We've got to do this again," Gary said as I was letting him off back at his house.

"Right," I said. "Give me a call." Before attempting the drive back to Chappaqua, and at the risk of letting the snow deepen, I stopped off at a late-hours diner for several black coffees.

19

Back at MU for the start of the winter term, it seemed almost as if I'd spent all of Christmas vacation in bars with Gary, singing and getting drunk.

We'd both come back a day early, riding the train together, because of the magazine. On the ride we met a girl also coming up early, because of the newspaper. Her name was Marge Baldwin and she was rather pretty. Gary took the lead with her—with my blessings, as I expected to be seeing Gwen for a while longer at least.

The bus finally pulled up in front of the Tower.

"Marge, may I help you with your bags?"

"Would you?"

"Gary, I'll see you at the office as soon as possible."

"Right. I won't be long." Letting Marge carry her train case and his satchel, he took both their suitcases and put hers in her room—another freshman cubicle—for her. "I guess that should do it."

"Thanks a lot, Gary."

"That's okay. How about dinner with me tonight?"

"I'd like to, but we've both got to work."

"I know. Look, what say whoever gets off first call the other, and we can work out the details then. Okay?"

"Okay. I'll be in the paper office."

"Right. And I'll be in the *Tumbrel* office. Do you know the number?"

"No, but I can find it."

"And I can find yours. Okay, we'll work it out."

"Okay. See you later."

"See you later."

I left my own stuff just inside the door of my suite, then went right to the office. Patty was already there.

"What took you so long?" she asked.

"Trains are always late. Have you been here long?"

"Couple of hours."

"Keeping busy, I trust."

"Yes, the proofs are in."

"Good."

"I've left a nice pile of them on your desk."

"Thanks . . . Did you have a good vacation?"

"Pretty good. You?"

"Not too bad. Gary and I hit the bars."

"Oh, that's right. You live just a short drive away from him, don't you?"

"Under half an hour."

"I can just see you two."

"Well, we were good customers. Anyhow, I'd better get going on those proofs."

"Have fun."

"You too." I sat down at the desk and started on the pile.

Gary came in shortly. "Hi, Patty. Have a good vacation?"

"Uh-huh. And I've already heard how you spent most of yours."

"Well . . ."

164

"Don't worry about it. Have some proofs."

"Thanks."

He sat down at his desk and got ready to work.

"After all," I said to him, "the sooner we get done, the sooner you can see Marge. That is what you're planning on doing, isn't it?"

"Well, yes."

"Okay then. Let's all dig in, for her sake."

We dug in, and after some time, with innumerable checkbacks to original manuscripts, got the proof out of the way.

"Duncan," Gary asked, "are you going to need me for anything else?"

"Not if Marge is free."

"Well, we've arranged that whoever is finished first will call the other."

"Call her. If necessary, I'm sure we can find something to keep you busy until she gets off."

"Thanks." He borrowed my phone book to find the number of the *Daily Bulletin* office, then borrowed my phone. ". . . Yes, please. Is Marge Baldwin there? . . . Thank you." Sitting on my desk, carefully not on the proofs, he took advantage of his waiting time to light a cigarette. "Hello, Marge? Gary . . . Yeah, I think they might be willing to let me go for the day . . . Fine. What time shall I stop by for you? . . . Sure. Do you know what's open yet? . . . No, but we'll find out. Six-thirty, then? . . . Okay, 'Bye for now." He hung up the phone. "As you heard, I'm meeting her at six-thirty. I've got plenty of time if there's anything else I can do."

"Well, I want to do a paste-up, but I can take that home. If you would, though, you could take the proofs back to the printshop on your way out."

"Sure thing."

Patty had just finished combining our three piles of corrected proof. Gary scooped them up. "So long, Patty. So long, Duncan."

We waved to him and watched him leave. Then Patty started packing her purse. I put the materials for the paste-up into a folder and stood up.

"Let me buy you dinner?" I said.

"Sure," she said.

I was just about to get ready for bed when Gary showed up.

"Thought I'd get a look at the paste-up."

"There it is." I indicated the living room table.

He went over and looked through it. "Looks good. You've been working on it all evening?"

"Most of the evening. I took Patty to dinner."

"Good."

"How was your date?"

"Kind of funny." He set himself down on the sofa and lit one of his perennial Camels.

I sat down in the armchair facing the sofa. "Well?"

"Well, I don't think I'll be seeing her again. It's funny. We had dinner, and afterwards we just sat and talked—didn't even have anything to drink. I never even thought of inviting her to my room or trying to invite myself to hers. She's bright, she's charming—you noticed that, I'm sure—but she's too goddam *nice*."

"What was that fine distinction between a *nice* girl and a *good* girl? I can never remember it."

"One of them goes home and then goes to bed and the other goes to bed and then goes home. I can't remember which is supposed to be which."

"Anyhow."

"Anyhow, there's something about her—I just don't think I'd do her any good."

"There's a little bit of bitch in every girl, just as there's a little bit of bastard in every guy. You've just got to seek it out."

He gave me a sour look. "Come on."

"No, really, I do think you're downgrading yourself a bit too much. And maybe she'd be a good influence on you."

"I don't know. I just don't think I'll be seeing her again."

"That," I said, "is entirely up to you."

"Well . . ." He got up and went to the table again. "The paste-up does look good."

So much for Marge Baldwin.

Gary met Connie Pearce at one of the club's mixer-parties, the kind that only paramours could attend as couples. It was a Friday evening just a short time into the new term. I skipped the party, as I already had a date but wasn't about to trade favours with her. It was a stand-up party, with dancing to records for those who wanted to.

Gary, drink in hand, was doing his standing-up off to one side of the room by a table spread with minor food-stuffs. Currently between cigarettes, he was sampling the potato chips and chip-dip. So far this evening he'd been doing more drinking than mixing, hadn't danced yet, and had talked only with fellow members and paramours he knew. Some new pairings-off had already taken place, but it was still fairly early.

"How's the dip?" A girl had come over to the table where he'd been standing by himself until now.

"Not bad." He stood aside to let her get at it. "I don't

believe we've been introduced—not that anyone ever is at these things."

"I know." She quickly ate her small piece of dipped chip. "I'm Connie Pearce."

"Gary Fort. How do you do."

"How do you do."

He bowed and she curtsied.

"God," he said, "I believe we've just brought a modicum of etiquette to this affair."

"Very good. What do we do next?"

"Well, I could offer you a cigarette." He brought out his pack of Camels. She was pretty good-looking, he was coming to realize.

"And I could accept." She took one and he lit it with the Zippo his resigned parents had given him as part of his Christmas. "Thank you."

"You're welcome." He lit one for himself too, of course. "Aren't these parties stupid?"

"Yes, but they're planned that way, you know."

"Really?"

"Of course," she said. "So that you can start a conversation by saying how stupid the party is."

"That's pretty clever."

"Very. The clubs know how to do things, and of course Tower knows best."

"Of course. We serve good chip-dip too."

She nodded. "With true *savoir-faire*."

"Very, very suavely. It's still a stupid party."

"I know." She laughed.

"I think I'd rather have non-stupid parties and take my chances at making conversation some other way. Maybe I'll have time to get used to them, though."

"You might. You're a freshman, aren't you?"

"How'd you guess?" He was in uniform with his white tags back on his shoulders.

168

"Intuition. You know, they say your freshman year either makes you or breaks you. You're still a virgin, so to speak."

"I suppose. Which did your freshman year do for you?"

"I'm not sure. One or the other, certainly, but I don't know which yet."

"Then you're still something of a virgin too. What year are you?"

"Junior. Do the wrinkles show?"

"Not in this light. Do you think you could dance without your cane?"

"I can try."

They stubbed out their cigarettes in an ashtray on the table and went to the cleared-for-dancing part of the room.

"I'm exhausted," he said as they retreated from the dancing area after several fast ones in succession. "You see, youth isn't everything."

"I never said it was."

"You must understand, of course, that on top of classes today I've had a hard day at the office."

"The office?"

"*Tumbrel*. Great White Father Duncan Chase didn't even make it here tonight."

"What do you do on the *Tumbrel?*"

"I'm sort of assistant to the assistant to the editor. Office boy, in other words. No, actually, I'm supposed to be editor of the frosh issue. And if Duncan ever gets a promotion of some kind, I suppose I've got a good chance of getting the whole burden for myself on a permanent basis."

"Very good."

"Yeah, I'm a very big tadpole in the pond. Dr. Clark always consults me before making decisions."

"I'm sure."

"How about a drink?"

"Okay."

"What do you like?"

"Surprise me."

"I'll try." He went and got two bourbon-and-waters from the bar, came back and handed her one. "Surprise."

She took a sip. "Good. Not too surprising, but good."

"I've failed."

"No, no. Apparently not at all." She pointed to the black term ribbon he now wore over his breast pocket.

"Oh, that." He had wondered about buying and wearing it, but had gathered that no one had any objection to term ribbons of any color. "Pure luck."

"Now, don't be bashful. I'm in the same range myself."

"Really?"

"Always have been."

"Good God. That's better than I'll probably do."

"Don't say that. You're still young."

They kept talking, drinking slowly, and dancing until close to midnight, the preset hour for dissolution of the party. Finally Gary considered and made his next move.

"You will pardon my youthful brashness, but why don't we have the next few drinks at my room?"

"Why don't we have them at my room?" she said. "It's probably bigger, and that'd save me the walk home later."

He spread his hands. "Whatever you like."

They waved their good-byes to the others and left the party.

"Ah, fresh air!" he said when they were out in the hall-way.

"Come on," she said.

Her room was bigger than his and had a kitchenette and some windows; otherwise was much the same.

"Very nice place you've got here."

"Thanks. You want to stick with bourbon?"

"Please."

She was soon back where he sat, with glasses.

"You were right," he said, "about coming here instead of my room. I don't have any ice cubes."

"You see?" She smiled and sat down across from him.

"Uh-huh . . . Very nice place. Good bourbon, too."

"Would you like some music?"

"Sure."

"What kind?"

"Surprise me."

"I'll try." She did, by putting a very noncommercial jazz side on her phonograph. When she came back she sat down next to him. They listened to the first band intensely; he occasionally made abstruse comments, jokingly, which she would answer with "Oh yes," or "Of course." Then the band ended and they were kissing, naturally enough.

The side ended and she pulled away. "I'm afraid I'm going to have to turn you out now. I've got all kinds of chores to do tomorrow morning."

"Do you have to?"

"Uh-huh. But we can do this again sometime."

"That's good. I'll call you tomorrow?"

"All right." She saw him to the door. They had their good nights and Parthian kisses. Then he went to his own room.

Although there was little physical resemblance, Connie reminded him somehow of Barb Tillman.

Saturday night Connie and Gary, after dinner together, were at a bar. They sat at a table with a pitcher between them, which was not in its first filling.

"What do you most want to do here?" she asked him.

"Let me think." He looked ceilingward for a couple of seconds, then back to her. "Graduate."

She laughed. "I guess that's what most everybody wants. I'll tell you, though, I want something else."

"What?"

"I want to execute somebody," she whispered.

"Really?"

"Yes. It doesn't matter who. I just want to know what it's like. I want to have done it."

"Well, you might, mightn't you?"

"I've always been in high range."

"You might."

"Do you think it's terrible of me?"

"I wouldn't know. I'm the freshman, remember." He smiled.

So did she. "Thanks. That's the one thing, you know. After that, I could hardly care what happened to my grades."

"Now, now. Can't afford to get slipshod."

"Well . . ."

From the bar they went to her room, after stopping off at Gary's for some of his records. She approved of his print.

After she'd put records on her phonograph and given him more of her bourbon, they spent more time together on her sofa. When he broached the ultimate topic in their dialogue, she just said, "Not tonight."

He didn't complain; the evening had gone pleasantly enough as it was.

"Duncan, how'd you like a wonderful girl?"

"What's the matter with her?" It was a Wednesday

night, after club meeting, and Gary and I were sitting in my suite.

"Nothing. It's just that I don't think she's right for me, and I don't want to see her go to waste."

"Okay, what's she like?"

"Her name's Constance Pearce, she's a junior in math, high range. You've met her."

"Uh-huh. Well . . ." I had mentioned to him a few days before that I'd stopped seeing Gwen. "Why do you say she's not right for you?"

"I don't know. I just think I've gotten out of my depth this time. Can't psych her out."

"Big deal. Sit back and maybe learn something."

"Nahh . . . Look, I really think she could get along with you. She warmed up to me appreciably after I told her I was on the *Tumbrel*, and I'm not much more than an office boy."

"Patience, as for that. As for the girl, you say she thinks she's gaining some kind of status by seeing a *Tumbrel* boy?"

"Apparently."

"Is that what's putting you off?"

"Not just that. I can't figure out exactly what she's after."

"Big deal again . . . So you just don't want her. Or have you already had her?"

"Once. She's pretty good."

"So you can tell by now. Very good."

"Okay—I suppose you can?"

"Only in extreme cases. Anyhow, you want me to take the responsibilities off your shoulders?"

"Uh-huh."

"Well, I guess I could try."

"Thanks."

173

"What's the deal?"

"There's no deal yet. I'll set it up as well as I can."

"Okay," I said, "let me know."

"I will."

"Connie, there's something I'm going to explain to you, and then something else I'm going to suggest. Will you bear with me?"

"What is it?" They were sitting together in one of the quiet bars the following Friday night. The evening had scarcely begun.

"Well . . . I think I ought to stop seeing you."

"Oh."

"It's not that I don't like you. I do, quite a lot. You know that."

She nodded. "I like you too."

"I can't really explain it very well. I just don't think I should keep seeing you."

". . . Is it the age difference or the class difference that's bothering you?"

"No, neither. I could feel the same way about a freshman."

"Well, that's something."

"Really, it just seems like we're going in different directions, and neither of us knows just which way the other is going."

"I didn't expect you to go so far as to marry me."

"I know. I never thought you had that in mind."

"Thanks. I see, you're just tired of me."

"No, certainly not. I couldn't get 'tired' of anyone in so short a time."

"Good for you."

"Okay, I've put it wrong. But what I'm trying to explain

174

is that I think we ought to end it. Do you understand? I really do think it's the best thing."

"I can't hold you against your will."

He paused to light a defensive cigarette. "I'm sorry, I really am."

"So am I."

"Look, I do feel I've got a certain obligation to you. I certainly can't make anything more than partial repayment, but that's what the suggestion's about."

"What is it?"

"You remember Duncan Chase? You met him at that party last week."

"Yes."

"Well, I've been talking to him and I know he'd like to see you. I've told him a little bit about you."

"Yes, I bet you have."

"Cut it out. Really, he would be a pretty good deal if you wanted to get something going. He's a junior, he's the editor of the *Tumbrel*, and he's in Tower, as you know. He's taught me practically everything I know."

"I see. You've sold me to him. What did you get for me?"

"Cut it out. I just thought the two of you might get along well."

"Very good." She brought out her cigarettes and received a light from him. "But I don't like deals like this."

"Will you just try this one?"

"Why?"

"Because I think it'd work out."

"Who for?"

"For you, dammit."

"Did anyone ever tell you you're a very nasty young man?"

"Not tonight."

"You are."

"Okay. I am. Will you try it?"

"All right, I'll try it. Bring on Duncan Chase. Connie is all ready to get caught on the rebound. Not much of a rebound, I'm afraid—but there wasn't much of a bound to begin with."

"I'm sorry. But I really think he'd be a lot better for you."

"We'll have to see about that."

"Connie? Duncan Chase."

"Hello, Duncan. I was expecting you to call."

"Gary told you?" I asked.

"Gary worked everything out, rather artlessly. But I won't let that prejudice me against you."

"Thanks. I'm afraid he thought you were more than he could handle."

"So he's passing me on to his guru. I'll make you a deal, Duncan. I won't try to 'handle' you if you won't try to 'handle' me."

"Agreed."

"Good. Well, I take it you're supposed to ask me out now."

"If it's all right with you. And please accept my apologies for Gary. I'm afraid he's still very young."

"Yes, I know. I didn't know just *how* young until last night."

"Give him time."

"Not my time, not any more."

I laughed. "I understand. Look, I think we both agree that this is a pretty stupid situation. Shall we see what we can do with it anyhow? How about dinner tonight?"

"All right."

"We can't disappoint the kid, after all."

"Let's leave that out of it."

"Certainly. Pick you up at six?"

"Fine."

The following day, Sunday afternoon, I was thinking about how I could make the situation more symmetrical. I'd always had a rather annoying matchmaker-impulse, and now two names kept coming together in my mind. Finally I turned to my telephone.

"Hello?"

"Hello, Nancy. How are you?"

"Hello, Duncan. All right. You?"

"Coping, as usual."

She laughed a little. "Your new issue is pretty good."

"Thanks. . . . There was something I wanted to ask you about. If I get out of line, tell me and I'll drop it."

"Sure. What is it?"

"There's a guy I'd like you to meet. Could you?"

"I've been having all first dates recently, if that's what you mean."

"That's what I mean. I think you could do him some good."

"I'm not a social worker, or an analyst."

"I know. I just think you might be a beneficial influence."

"Wonderful. Could he do me any good?"

"I don't know. You'd have to see him and find out."

"All right, what's he like?"

"Well, he's a freshman, very pleasant most of the time, and I suppose he's reasonably good looking."

"Uh-huh."

"The age difference doesn't bother you, does it?"

"Not if it doesn't bother him. You were a year *older* than me."

"True. Okay. I think he's a pretty good guy—I wouldn't be talking to you about him otherwise. His name's Gary Fort."

"Oh yes. He had a story in the new issue, didn't he?"

"Yes."

"It was pretty good. Almost like the stuff you used to write."

"Thanks. Anyhow, will you let me try to arrange a meeting?"

"Sure. Doesn't he know about this?"

"No, it's all my idea. I hope he won't mind—he'd better not."

She laughed. "He isn't seeing anyone currently, is he?"

"No, not now. You can get his complete amorous history from him, if you want. He'd probably tell it more interestingly than I would."

"Say, is he your protégé by any chance?"

"More or less."

"I thought so."

"Forgive me?"

"Sure. You know you're awful, don't you?"

"I know."

"All right. Let me know when to expect the big phone call."

"Will do. And Nancy—thanks."

"Any time, Duncan, any time."

Then I called Gary. "I figured you'd want a progress report from me."

"Yeah. Did you take her out?"

"Dinner at the Tower Room. The works. I figured she deserved at least that much."

"How do you mean?"

"Well, we spent most of the evening apologizing to each other for you."

"I'm sorry."

"That's all right."

"Thanks. And after the apologies, how'd it go?"

"All right. I expect we'll be seeing each other again."

"Good. Do you think she might be an acceptable replacement for Gwen?"

"That's a hell of a way to put it, but yes, I do think she might be an acceptable replacement. Maybe a good bit more than acceptable. Are you happy now?"

"I guess so. Yeah, sure."

"Good, because I've got a surprise for you."

"Huh?"

"No, Connie and I did not trade favours last night. But you might—you never know."

"What?"

"Well, I didn't want to leave a debt outstanding, so I thought, since you've given me a girl, I'd give you a girl. It's all right—I've already checked with her."

"Wait a second."

"There's nothing wrong with her. I've checked her references. Very pretty, intelligent, charming. She even cooks."

"Duncan . . ."

"Now, Gary, I just wanted to be sure all our transactions balanced out. Since Connie looks pretty good to me, I thought I'd do you a favor in return."

"How do you know this girl?"

"She's an old friend. I can vouch for her personally."

"How so?"

"You'll just have to take my word for it."

"Thanks."

"Quite all right. When shall I tell her to expect your call?"

"Give me a little while to brood. Tell her five o'clock."

"Fine."

"I don't have to go through with this, you know."

"Agreed, you don't. But you're going to want to know what you're passing up, and I couldn't tell you. I'll tell her five o'clock."

"All right. Hey, you haven't told me her name yet."

"Oh, that's right. Nancy Sanford. Great girl."

20

He had it planned. It was set for six-thirty. He had enough money with him to cover the Tower Room if the situation warranted it. If not, there were other places. If it really looked bad, he'd steer her to the second-floor cafeteria or one of the snack bars and that could be the end of it. When he saw her, there was no longer any question—it would be the Tower Room.

"Ready to go?"

"Uh-huh." She locked her room and took his arm.

They got their table. It would be a couple of minutes before the waiter would come.

"Would you like a drink?" Gary asked.

"Yes, please. I'll have a gibson."

"What's that?"

"It's just a martini with an onion instead of an olive."

"Okay. Sounds interesting." He nodded.

She brought her cigarettes out of her purse. She had them in one of those pack-holder cases. They were "cork" —tipped filters—Marlboros or Winstons, he guessed. He lit her cigarette, then drew out and lit one of his Camels.

"I read your story in the new *Tumbrel*," she said. "I like it."

"Thanks. It was fun to do."

"That's when it's best, isn't it—when it's fun?"

He nodded. "Definitely. Do you write?"

"No, I just like to read about writing. Have you been doing anything more?"

"Not really. Just notes. I've been in the middle of a dry spell. My *Tumbrel* work's all editorial these days."

"You're on the staff?"

"Office boy, more or less. But it's fun."

"What do you think of Duncan?"

"I think he's a pretty good guy. What else could I say— he's put me on the magazine and gotten me into his club."

"Then you're another Tower. He must think quite a bit of you."

"I guess so."

"What would you say if you didn't think you were obligated to him?"

"I'd say he's a pretty decent guy. He's been my drinking buddy for a while now, and I wouldn't say that's because of any sense of obligation. He and I just get along—most of the time. We have, just about ever since we met. Why? What do you think of him?"

"I like him."

The waiter came with menus.

"Two gibsons, please," Gary said.

The waiter nodded and left.

"What would you like?" Gary asked over the menus.

"The beef Bourguignon, I think."

"Sounds good."

They managed to get the minor details as well worked out by the time the waiter returned with their drinks.

"What do you know," Gary said after his first sip. "An onion-flavored martini. Okay."

She smiled. "I suppose there are some very subtle reasons for preferring them to martinis. I just like cocktail onions."

He smiled. "They're good, aren't they."

She picked up her cigarette from the ashtray. "You know, I was wondering what Duncan was doing when he called me. The way he sounded, he was trying to fix me up with some kind of social basket-case."

"Really? I certainly had no idea of what he was up to, didn't know what you'd be like. I thought he was mad at me and was trying to put me into some kind of tight spot."

"But you aren't now, are you?"

"I'll tell you, I am. You see, I've got this problem about ordering wines. Do you know anything about it?"

"No, not really. If you'd rather skip the wine, it's fine with me."

"I always feel kind of guilty about ordering something I don't know how to appreciate. If it's all the same to you—there's Burgundy in the entree, after all. No point in getting stewed before you're through eating."

"None at all. It's fine with me."

"Okay."

"You didn't really have to take me here, you know, either."

"I wanted to, after I saw you."

"Thank you."

"You're welcome. I hope you don't mind being seen here with me."

"Not at all. Really."

"Thanks."

They finished their cigarettes and drinks in relative silence, not uncomfortably.

"Very good onion," she said.

"Mine was perhaps even a great onion," he said. "Wonder what year it was?"

She laughed.

The waiter came back with shrimp cocktails. "Your wine order?"

"We'll skip the wine, thanks," Gary said.

They had the meal, with the usual unobtrusive piano music. Then coffee, brandy, and more cigarettes.

"What brand are those?" he asked.

"Marlboro."

"I was smoking those for a while. They seem harsh in large quantities."

"Well, you've just got to learn not to smoke more than two cigarettes at once."

"Yeah, that's something to work on . . . I like the Camels pretty well."

"I can take one once in a while, but not as a steady diet. Why do you stick to a non-filter?"

"Death wish? I don't know, they seem to taste better. These, at least. I'm no expert, of course. Only took up the habit this fall."

"Took up?"

"Yes. One morning I just bought myself a pack of cigarettes and taught myself how to inhale."

"Must be death wish."

"I guess it's not impossible. I'm up to close to two packs a day."

"That's awful. I think it's bad when I come near one. You really ought to cut down."

"I suppose. All I need is a reason."

"There's always your health."

"Yes, but considerations of health seem more or less suspended here."

"I know."

"Say, I hope you won't be offended by my asking, but it is Sunday night and all. Do you have to study tonight?"

"I really do have to, now that you mention it. That doesn't mean I wouldn't like to see you again."

"Thanks. Would Friday be all right?"

"Be fine."

"Good. I'll find out what'll be going on. The club might be having a party. I'll be in touch."

"Fine."

"Well, shall we head out? I've got books I should be pounding too."

She nodded.

They paused at her door.

"Did—did Duncan tell you I used to be his paramour?"

"No, he didn't. He just said you were an old friend."

"That's true by now. I just wanted you to know."

"He certainly can't mind."

"No, but I was afraid you might."

"Not if you don't."

"No," she said.

Then she had the door unlocked and opened. The movement to kiss was a mutual one.

"Good night, Gary."

"Good night, Nancy."

He saw her again Friday night and kept on seeing her; it wasn't what I had expected. I was seeing Connie. Every so often the four of us ran into each other as couples but never spent much time that way. We never doubled. The reasons were that Connie's opinion of Gary remained fairly low, and that I didn't want Gary and Nancy to think I was trying to supervise them in any way. I did see each of the three individually, though: Gary at the office and club meetings, Connie other evenings, and Nancy at odd moments in between, sometimes by chance and sometimes because she wanted to talk to me.

One Wednesday night Gary and I were off to one side at a club meeting.

"You know," he said, "I was, shall we say, apprehensive when you first arranged for me to meet Nancy. Will you let me apologize for that?"

"Sure, if you want."

"Thanks. And thanks for thinking of the whole thing to begin with. It's working out fine."

"Good. I'm glad to hear it."

"She's told me that she used to be your paramour. I think I owe you some extra thanks because of that."

"Believe me, it's all right."

One afternoon a little later, Nancy stopped up to see me.

"Drink?" I asked.

"Okay."

"Gimlet?"

"Sure." She didn't tell me that she rarely drank gimlets any more, or that she'd recently acquired a taste for bourbon.

"What's up?" I said as I handed her her drink.

"I wanted to thank you."

I sat down opposite her with my own gimlet. "Thank me?"

"Yes. I never thought you'd do anything like that—like what you did."

"Neither did I, until I did it. It's okay."

"Thanks . . . I'm not being the schoolgirl about this, I know I'm not."

"You never were."

She nodded, then looked up at me suddenly. "Duncan, I love him. I hope you don't mind my telling you."

I nodded. "I don't mind. I couldn't. Believe me, I don't mind."

She smiled. "He's a lot like you."

I laughed. "But not too much, I hope. Nancy, this is the kind of thing I'd hoped for for you. Really."

"Thanks."

"For him too."

"Duncan, you're not awful at all."

"Now, *that* I can't believe."

"I can . . . Duncan, there's one thing I've got to ask you to do."

"You name it."

"All right, please don't tell Gary about the way my grades have been going."

"I didn't know anything about it. Are they bad?"

"Not very good. Fall was way down."

"I'm sorry. I won't mention it to him."

"Thanks. It's the one thing I can't tell him about."

I knew that she had seen him in uniform, had seen his black term-ribbon. "I understand."

"We've never discussed grades, somehow. I think I'd rather lie than tell him. I think it'd be better that way."

"Probably. At any rate, don't worry about me spilling it. This term will pick up, won't it?"

"It ought to. I've been studying very hard lately, and I'm going to keep on. There's no reason for him to think I haven't always studied hard."

"What happened in the fall?"

"I don't know. I just didn't do much of anything. For a while I was drinking too much, until I got scared of it."

"Nancy . . ."

"I know. There's no excuse." She was shaking her head. "But I think I can fix it."

"Good. I think you can too, if you want to."

"I want to, Duncan. Believe me, I want to."

21

Nancy was something new to Gary. One evening at her room, he was about to put a record on the phonograph, a jazz trumpeter with strings.

"You've played that a lot recently, haven't you?"

"I like it."

"Would you do me a favor?"

"Sure."

"Please don't play that again tonight."

"Why not?"

She came over to him and took his hand. "Because I don't want any canned sentimentality between us. We shouldn't need it."

"Okay." He put the record down.

She kissed him, a momentary brush. "Play something new. It should be new every time."

"It is." He kissed her harder, then found a different record to play, one of hers that he had never heard. "This all right?"

"Fine." She kissed him again.

Gary moved in with Nancy two days before Connie moved in with me. There was no question at the Mail

Room when he asked to have his mail delivered to her room. Their life together was . . . no single word in my vocabulary could be adequate. They both had eight-o'clock classes. They both got up each weekday morning at seven and amiably shared the bathroom. She fixed coffee and orange juice while he was in the shower. He ate a bowl of cold cereal while she was in the shower, and they worked it to have the orange juice and coffee—as much breakfast as she ever took—together. They parted for classes but returned to the room during free hours—the standing rule was studying during them. Time was short for lunch. She usually fixed sandwiches, sometimes with canned soup, and with them they drank milk. After the end of classes in the afternoon, Gary usually had work at the office, and she studied in the room and prepared dinner. She liked to cook, and dinner was the elaborate meal of the day. And he soon had discovered dishes that he could fix and enjoyed doing.

They split the grocery bills down the middle, but Gary sometimes surprised her by buying the makings of fancy touches. He bought a paperback book about wines and kept it at the office, so that one night (after having asked at lunch what she had planned for dinner) he was able to bring home exactly the right Bordeaux, a Medoc, Château Lafite-Rothschild. He brought the book home for her too, and after that they began having wine with the evening meal with some frequency.

Sunday through Monday evenings they studied together, one at the desk and the other on the sofa, with music playing below the level of distraction. On weekend evenings there would always be a film, a play, or a club party. Weekend mornings were for sleeping late. Saturday afternoons were for cleaning the room—and Gary found himself driven out with a shopping list. Sunday afternoons were for laziness, sitting in the room and reading or walking together outdoors. There was almost always snow on the ground, sometimes quite a bit, and they both enjoyed it.

He was the one who suggested that they declare themselves paramours. "I am living with you, after all."

She nodded. "So we don't need to declare ourselves. What use would it have?"

"We could go to the club mixer-parties."

"To watch everybody else trying to play quarter horse? You aren't charged for parties you don't go to, and there are enough of the other kind."

"Okay, I just thought you might like it better if we were declared."

"Really, there'd be no point in it."

"Okay. If you don't want to, it's okay by me."

He noticed that she was carefully taking her pills.

His smoking went down to a little under a pack a day and he started writing again. He showed me tantalizing bits of the thing he was working on—set at MU, picaresque, plotted as if at random. It had only a satiric resemblance to reality, it was good-natured, and it was funny. The first bit I saw I immediately slated for publication. It seemed as if the thing could go on forever without faltering.

Paramours' Day for the winter quarter came and went. Gary never had time to look at himself in the mirror.

"Want to stop over for a while?" I asked Gary one Wednesday night as we were leaving a club meeting.

"Okay. I'll want to call Nancy, though."

"No problem." We were both at least relatively sober. It apparently took less alcohol now for each of us to relax.

"Are you decent?" I called through the door of my suite. "I've got company."

"Sure."

We went inside.

"Hi, Connie."

"Hi, Gary." Their little feud was definitely over by now.

"Were you studying?" I asked.

"Yes, but I can move to the bedroom. Don't worry." She excused herself and moved her books to the other room.

"Beer, Gary?"

"Thanks."

I got a couple from the refrigerator and we sat down with them. "Connie, you want a beer?" I called as an afterthought.

"No thanks, not right now."

"Okay." Then I readdressed myself to Gary. "Pretty good meeting tonight." The club had taken in two more freshmen.

"Yeah. Stokes does all right with those monologues."

"I'll tell you a secret. He gets all his material from those Robert Orban books."

"But he still delivers it well."

"True."

"Hey, I've got to call Nancy."

"You know where the phone is."

He went to it. "Hi, honey . . . Yeah, the meeting was fine . . . Say, I'm up here at Duncan's for beers. I won't be in for a little while yet . . . Okay, fine . . . See you later. G'bye."

"She didn't mind, did she?"

"No, no trouble." He sat back down again. "I don't think she would have minded if I hadn't called."

"How do you mean?"

"Well, she never seems to require anything from me. You know, I suggested that we declare ourselves paramours. But she said it wasn't necessary."

"She's probably right."

"I know, but it startled me. She's like that. She has yet to ask me for anything."

"And you're complaining?"

"Hell, no. I'm just having a little trouble getting used to it."

"Do you act the same way towards her?"

"I try to. It's really pretty good that way."

"Sure."

"Duncan, I should thank you again. I love her. It's like it's never been before."

I nodded, then took a long sip from my beer. "Hey, what say I get out the slot-racers?"

"Fine."

I interrupted Connie briefly to get the board from the bedroom closet, then set it up in the living room. We ran race after race, exchanging cars and tracks, and got fresh beers a couple of times.

Finally Connie came back out. "Duncan, I'm going to bed now."

"Okay," I said.

"I'd better get going," Gary said. "Got an eight o'clock in the morning."

"Yeah," I said, "I think it's about time for me to turn in too."

"Thanks for the beers," he said at the door.

"Any time," I said. "Good night."

"G'night." He left, and I put the beer cans in the wastebasket, put the miniature Jaguar and Corvette back into their cigar box, and went to join Connie.

On a Saturday morning two weeks from term finals, Gary woke up gradually to see Nancy, with her robe on, working at the kitchenette.

"What are you doing?" he asked her.

"I'm making breakfast, silly."

"Come here."

"Why?"

"Come here."

"But I'm fixing the orange juice."

"Come here."

With a pleasantly annoyed expression, she came over and sat by him on the bed. "Now what's the matter with you?"

He pulled her down to him.

"Let me shut off the coffee."

He obediently released her. She went and turned off the burner under the coffee pot, then came back, took off her robe, and slipped in between the covers.

He had taken his shower and was just finishing getting dressed. She was fully clothed now and was pouring the coffee and setting out his cereal and milk.

He went to the table and kissed her neck. "Have I told you yet today that you're great?"

"Drink your coffee."

"You're great," he said as he sat down.

"Drink your coffee." She took a sip of hers.

Then the klaxon went off.

"On Saturday?" he said over the noise.

"It's been done before."

They got up from the table. The klaxons in the hall were slightly different in tone, just as loud as inside. She slipped her hand into his and they started for the Main Auditorium.

The halls were more and more crowded as they went along. Many people were in bathrobes and slippers. At the doors of the Auditorium were the floor supervisors with their tally-counters. A few of these were in robes instead of street clothes. Inside, there again were the circularly arranged seats and the floor space at the center with just the desk and microphone and the guillotine. She squeezed his hand as they entered and he gave answering pressure.

They took seats near at hand, at the periphery. The room filled more slowly this time, because of the day and hour—it wasn't yet noon.

The faculty member chosen at random to be the administrator now came forward. The floor supervisors went into their huddle to get the count, then closed the doors and stood before them. The klaxons stopped.

The administrator could be seen blowing into the microphone, but no air-rushing noise could be heard. Another faculty member came forward and made adjustments, blew once and got it to work, then got out of the way again.

The administrator began with a name. "Nancy B. Sanford."

Gary's head jerked to the side. Nancy looked very tired, but smiled briefly and squeezed his hand. He gave the answering squeeze. She kissed him once, then stood up and let go of his hand.

He started to get up, but without words she indicated that he was to remain seated. He sat halfway at the edge of the seat, his hands clenched to it, as she walked down to the center, slowly, almost disdainfully.

"Nancy B. Sanford," the administrator said, "Your name has been selected at random from those of students whose grades have fallen below the minimum acceptable level. Do you understand?"

She nodded once.

"Constance J. Pearce," the administrator said. For an instant Gary had thought it was going to be his name.

Gary's eyes stayed on Nancy, not on Connie's walk down to the center.

"Constance J. Pearce," the administrator said, "Your name has been selected at random from those of students whose grades are within the highest range. Do you understand?"

Connie nodded once, then she and Nancy took their places. Connie pulled the cord and it was over in an instant.

The floor supervisors came down to the center and quickly removed Nancy and Connie. "Dismissed," the administrator said, and walked off.

Students started to get up and leave. Gary could only dig his nails into his seat and shut his eyes tight.

PART THREE

22

After it was over, I didn't try to go to Connie. I was in my own state of shock, although I'd known of this possibility, and I knew that Connie could take care of herself—and I didn't care.

I remained in my seat long after most of the other students had left. When Nancy had been walking down to the center I had wanted to stop her, to stop the whole thing somehow. But her manner, the way she carried herself, had told me I mustn't. Now I was sitting there, my hands tight on my seat, not daring to move any part of myself. It wasn't that I thought I might be sick—being sick is a reaction to something impersonal. It was that I feared that if I were to move, I would instantly and irrevocably lose whatever sanity I had.

Finally the room was nearly empty. A few floor supervisors were down at the front, dismantling the machine in order to put it away until next time. Then I saw Gary, still in his seat a little way around the circle from me.

I made my way through the seats to him.

"Duncan. God . . ."

"I know, I know. Come on." I helped him up and steered him toward an exit.

"She never told me she was in low range. She never told me."

He leaned on me like a drunkard. I got him onto an elevator and up to my suite. "Gary, I think you'd better get some sleep now. Okay?"

"Okay."

"You go in there." I pointed him toward the bedroom. I went into the bathroom and got a glass of water and some pills for him from the medicine cabinet.

"What're those?"

"Sedative." I'd had them around ever since Heath had gotten the ax. "Come on, take them."

He gulped them down convulsively with the water.

"Try to relax now."

"Duncan, she never told me."

"I know. Try to sleep." I left the room and shut the door, leaving him lying on his back. When I checked on him a few minutes later he was out. I closed the bedroom door again and sat down in the living room.

Connie came in. Her face was pale, but apart from that she looked much as she usually did.

I said nothing.

She sat down opposite me and folded her hands in her lap.

"Gary's in the bedroom," I finally said. "I got him to take some sleeping pills."

She nodded. We sat. "Is it unforgiveable?" she said after a while.

"What?" My voice was coming out flat.

"That I wanted to do it."

"Are you satisfied?"

"No, I feel a little sick. Duncan, I'm sorry it was Nancy, I really am."

"So am I. Hell, I'm sorry it was anyone."

"I didn't even know she was in low range. The coincidence . . ."

"You couldn't enjoy it because it was someone you knew?"

"Duncan . . ."

I didn't feel like trying to console her. We sat.

"Duncan, is there anything I can do?"

"Yes. Move out."

She stood up and started getting her luggage out of a closet. I didn't bother to watch. The telephone rang. I went over to the desk and answered it. "Yes?"

"Duncan Chase?"

"Yes."

"This is Edmund West. I was administrator for the Self-Discipline Lesson today. Nancy Sanford indicated you as her Student Executor."

"Yes." I'd filled out one of those cards myself when I was in low range. I'd named Patty then as my Student Executor.

"I have a key to her room for you if you'd like to take charge of her effects. The room has to be ready for reoccupancy within three days, you know."

"I know. And I think I've already got a key."

"I've got one here for you if you don't. And Miss Sanford's instructions for you." He gave me the room number of an administrative office.

"Yes, thank you. I'll be down in a few minutes."

Connie was silently going in and out of the bedroom to pack her things. I looked at Gary once more to make sure he was sleeping through it, then left the room.

I had never had Associate Professor Edmund West for a course, but I had heard that he was a brilliant scholar and an excellent teacher. Right now he impressed me as a fool.

"Here's the key if you want it," he said, "and this is—instructions, I suppose." He handed me a standard white envelope, sealed, with my name written on it.

"Probably," I said as I took the key and envelope. I hadn't wanted to go through Gary's pockets looking for a key that might or might not be there. "Thank you."

I went up to Nancy's room. The bed was unmade. On the table were cups of coffee, glasses of orange juice, a box of dry cereal, a bowl, a spoon, and a bottle of milk. I closed the door behind me and locked it for some reason. I sat down at the desk.

The envelope contained a single sheet of white notebook paper. It was dated two days after Gary's moving in with her. It said:

> "Duncan,
>   I hope you don't mind my giving you this job. There just wasn't anyone else I would have wanted to do it.
>   There shouldn't be any big problems involved. Please send everything reuseable to my parents (address below). Sale of my textbooks should cover the shipping costs. Throw out anything else—the obvious junk—and please don't let Gary have any souvenirs.
>   Thanks.
>
> Nancy"

With the address of her parents in California, that was it. The handwriting was clear and steady.

I got up from the desk, dumped the coffee and orange juice down the sink drain, put the milk back into the refrigerator and the cereal into the cupboard, and left all the dishes in the sink.

Then I started going through the desk, thinking there might be papers she would want disposed of before Gary could see them. There were none. No diary, no personal notebook, no personal papers at all beyond a few receipts and a box of canceled checks, all prosaic enough. Everything else was course-related. She apparently was not a letter-saver. I dumped all the papers into the wastebasket and made a mental note to take it to the incinerator.

I looked through the closet and the dresser drawers. About half the stuff was Gary's. As I'd pretty much expected, there was a key in the top dresser drawer, with "1814" stamped on it. It would help.

I was going to need some cartons for shipping Nancy's things. I could probably get them from one of the shops downstairs. Gary's stuff could be moved back to his own room easily enough. There would maybe be a few things whose ownership would be doubtful. I decided that whenever I might be in doubt, I would resort to the wastebasket.

It was just getting started that was difficult. After sitting there at the desk for several moments, I picked up the telephone and called Patty.

"Duncan. I've been trying to call you."

I grunted in vague affirmation. "I'm in Nancy's room. She named me her Student Executor."

"Do you want me to help?"

"That's why I called."

"I'll be right over. How's Gary?"

"Out. I gave him some of my sleeping pills. He should be all right for a while."

"I guess that's good. I'll be over in just a couple of minutes."

"Fine. Thanks."

"It's okay, really. See you soon."

"See you." I put down the phone and stayed sitting there at the desk. I was glad I'd gotten rid of the coffee and orange juice.

Patty wasn't more than a couple of minutes in coming. She knocked on the door and I unlocked it and let her in.

She smiled hesitantly at me; I couldn't help smiling back. I showed her the note after our little smiles had passed.

She nodded after reading it. "Why don't you go down and sell the books and see about getting some packing cartons. I'll see about sorting things out up here."

"Okay." I started to gather the obvious texts off the shelves. "Which ones are hers?"

"Name should be on the flyleaves."

"Of course." I found the ones with Nancy's signature inside and gathered them up under one arm. "See you later."

Patty waved and I left. There was little traffic in the halls and I had an elevator to myself. The clerk in the Book Exchange seemed very bored. I didn't waste any words in getting the usual fifty per cent of new list.

"Have you got any cartons I could have?" I remembered to ask.

"I think so. Wait a minute. How many?"

"As many as you can spare. I'll bring back the ones I don't use."

"I'll see." He went to a stockroom, came back a minute or two later with several large cardboard cartons.

I took the cartons and money back up to Nancy's room. "Think these'll be enough?"

"Should be fine," Patty said.

"Good." I took the book money from my pocket—I'd put it there rather than in my wallet, so that it wouldn't be confused with my own—and set it down on the desk.

"Will that cover it?"

"I think so," I said. "I'll send whatever's left to her parents."

Patty nodded. "I've got this pile of Gary's stuff here on the bed. If you want to run it to his room, that should be it."

"Might as well." I borrowed a couple of the cartons and dumped the pile of clothing and personal effects into them. For an instant it seemed that Gary was the one who had gotten the ax.

"You have his key, don't you?"

"Yeah." The key to 1814 was in my pocket. With Patty holding the door for me, I picked up one of the full cartons and carried it out. "Be back."

At Gary's room I set the carton down to unlock the door. Inside, there was a thick film of dust all over everything. I emptied out the contents of the carton onto the sofa and went back for the other one.

"Be back," I said to Patty again, going out with the second carton. I dumped it out onto the floor in Gary's room, puffed a few times, then locked the room up again and took the carton back.

Patty had already filled two cartons with Nancy's clothing. "I'll need some labels, and probably some twine."

I nodded and went back downstairs to get them. When I got back I closed up the cartons Patty had filled—using paper tape, a helpful afterthought, along with the twine— and labeled them with the address from the bottom of the instruction sheet.

"Can I help you with the rest of the stuff?" I asked. "No use mailing any of them until they're all ready."

"Sure, if you want to."

So I helped her fold dresses and skirts and sweaters and put them carefully into the cartons. We packed Nancy's record-player and clock-radio between layers of clothing.

Finally all the cartons were ready to go, the ones containing the breakables marked "fragile." I called the University Post Office and they said they'd send a man right up.

The wastebasket was full by now, with half-used cosmetics and food added to the papers from the desk. I took it down the hall to the incinerator and got back just as the man from the post office arrived. He had a two-wheeled carrier and a small spring scale.

With a minimum of words, apparently due to embarrassment, he hefted each of the cartons in turn on the hook of the scale. He told me the charges and I paid him out of the money on the desk. Then he put the cartons on the carrier and started to leave. "I . . . saw it today. I'm sorry."

"Thanks," I said.

The room looked pretty bare by now. Even the blankets from the bed had been packed—and now shipped. Patty had folded up the University-owned sheets and left them on top of the mattress.

"I guess all I've got to do now is organize Gary's stuff for him."

"No," Patty said. "You go get yourself something to eat. You've had a much harder time of it today than I have, I know. You give me Gary's key and I'll take care of it."

"I shouldn't let you."

"Yes you should. Come on, now."

"Thanks." I handed her the key. "You've been great today, really."

"You just get yourself some supper. And let me know how Gary is."

"I will. Thanks again."

"Go on, go on."

I smiled, perhaps a bit sheepishly, and left. I went down to a snack bar and had two hamburgers and a cup of coffee.

23

After the hamburgers, I went back to my suite. I looked into the bedroom again to check on Gary. He wasn't there.

I called his room.

"Duncan?"

"Yeah, Patty. Has Gary been there?"

"No. What's the matter?"

"He's not here. I've got to see if I can find him. I'll talk to you later."

I tried calling Nancy's room. The phone rang at the other end but nobody answered.

The next place to try was obvious. Not trusting the phone, I ran out and up to Connie's room, taking the stairs rather than waiting for an elevator.

I tried the door without knocking. It was unlocked and I went inside.

"Duncan!" Connie said. She was off to one side of the room. Gary stood at the other, smiling just a little bit.

"Gary, what the hell do you think you're doing?"

"I'm going to tear her apart, that's all. Don't try to stop me."

I moved between them. "Don't move."

"Didn't she ever tell you about her greatest ambition —to perform an execution? Well, now it's my turn."

"Gary, you lay one finger on her and I'll make it so that they'll have to scrape you off the walls." Right now I felt like I could have done it.

Tableau: Connie on one side of the room, about to go hysterical, Gary on the other side, just about ready to call my maybe-bluff. Me in the middle.

"I know for a fact that she's sorry it was Nancy," I said. "I mean that. And you know damn well that regardless of whether she wanted to or not, they never would have let her get out of doing the execution, once her number'd come up."

"Shut up, Duncan."

"You shut up. It's not her fault one way or the other. If you want to go tear President Clark apart instead, that's something else."

"I'm not listening to you, Duncan."

"Fine, because I don't want to try to argue with you. If you want a fight, I'll give you one."

So we had one. He came out with a kick aimed for my groin. I managed to dodge it and hit the underside of his nose with the side of my hand. He reeled backward and put his hands to his face.

"More?" I asked.

His hands came down from his face and he started to edge forward again.

Then Connie slipped something into my hand. I realized what it was and felt for the button. A six-inch blade flicked out.

Gary backed off again.

I moved back to clear the doorway. "Out."

Gary edged to the door and out it.

"Keep your door locked," I said to Connie as I went out the door, not taking my eyes off Gary. At the last instant of door-closing, I tossed the knife in at the floor behind me.

"Thanks, Duncan," Connie said. Then I heard the lock click behind me.

"Now," I said, "do you want to take up where we left off?"

Gary shook his head.

"That wasn't a very fair fight, I know. Those pills always leave you a bit groggy. You were actually pretty lucky. Who knows what she would have done to you if she'd been able to get to the knife before I got there? Your nose all right?"

He nodded. "Hurts, though."

"That's to be expected. Come on, we're going back to my suite."

He followed me meekly enough. I closed the door behind us and waved him to a chair. Then I went to the bar, got a bottle of bourbon, and set it down beside him. "If you want to drink, that'd be a little bit better."

"Thanks." He took up the bottle, opened it, and took a horribly large slug. It made him cough a bit, but he took another.

I sat there and watched him get drunk, with just one short intermission to call Patty and tell her everything was more or less in hand. I knew that this probably wasn't the right way to be handling him, but I wasn't about to call in the floor supervisors to help, even though they might be a little more experienced with such cases.

He was silent at first, but he rapidly got deep into the bottle and started talking. It was "she never told me" again. It soon got so that I could hardly understand what he was saying.

Then he started to be sick. I got him into the bathroom, if not as far as the bowl. He was spewing all over the floor, all liquid—he hadn't yet had anything to eat that day.

I held him up with his open mouth aimed at the toilet bowl. He emptied his stomach and kept on heaving, dry now. He spat and hacked and couldn't bring up anything more but phlegm.

Finally he stopped. I made him drink a little water and that stayed down all right. I got him out of the bathroom, into the bedroom, and stretched out on the bed.

"You try to sleep now."

He made efforts at nodding.

"It's okay. Just relax." I got the bedroom wastebasket and set it on the floor beside his head.

He was murmuring something I couldn't understand at all.

"Relax, relax. Go to sleep."

I turned out the light, shut the door, and left him. I got a mop and bucket from the supply closet down the hall and cleaned up the bathroom. Then I turned off the lights and tried to go to sleep on the living room sofa.

The next afternoon, Sunday, I woke up later than Gary. Opening my eyes, I saw him sitting in the chair across from the sofa, with a bottle and a glass.

"Well," I said, "I see you have no trouble finding things for yourself."

"You don't mind, do you?"

"Of course not, if that's what you want to do. How'd you sleep?"

"All right—except for the dreams."

I nodded, then slowly got up. "What time is it?"

"About one."

I grunted. I was sitting on the edge of the sofa now. "You been up long?"

"About half an hour. I'm trying to kill my hangover."

I put my shoes on and went to the bathroom. I got a pill from the medicine cabinet and handed it to him when I got back. "Here, take this. Then I won't have to worry about you."

"What is it?"

"A vitamin pill. Go on."

He shrugged, then palmed the pill to his mouth and washed it down with a long sip from his glass. It looked like he was at least cutting it with water now.

I got myself a shower and shave and fresh clothes, then started making coffee. "You want some?"

"No thanks."

"No, I wouldn't think so." I poured myself a cup and carried it over to my desk. "Well, I've got some work to do. You feel free to drink as much as you like, so long as you're fairly quiet about it."

"Thanks."

"And try not to barf again, or you'll have to clean it up yourself."

"Was I sick?"

"Most definitely." I addressed myself to some studying, ignoring Gary's apologies.

He sat there with his glass and bottle, only occasionally getting up for water or to use the bathroom. I kept the corner of my eye on him and actually managed to get some work done.

It was about six when Patty came by. "I thought maybe I could take you to dinner."

"Thanks, but I don't know about leaving Gary alone."

"I think he should be all right. He's a big boy."

"But he's a big boy with a lot of booze in him. Gary, will you be all right if we go out to dinner?"

"Sure."

"Will you please just stay here—don't go anywhere?"

"Sure."

"Okay, then. We'll see you a little later."

"See you."

Patty and I left. We agreed on the large cafeteria as being adequate to our present needs and got one of the window-tables, despite the crowding of the place at that hour.

Over the meal I told her again about the previous evening's action, filling in the details I hadn't had time for before.

"Sounds like he was in a bad way."

"He was."

"What about Connie?"

"I wouldn't know."

"But you did go with her once."

"Yes, but I've been having to think deep humanitarian thoughts to come to her defense as much as I have already. I just don't want to."

Patty nodded. "I think I understand."

We took a long time over dinner. I was one of those people who feel better for talking a thing out, and she knew it. I went over the previous day with her, again and again.

When we got back to my suite, Gary was passed out in his chair. She took the glass and rinsed it out at the sink while I put the bottle away.

"Should we move him?" she asked.

"I don't think so. He should be all right where he is."

"Okay."

"Tonight," I said, "I can sleep in my own bed."

She smiled. "Well, I'd better be going, I'm afraid I've got homework waiting up for me."

"Me too." We went back to the door.

"Duncan, I think I understand how you feel. I never knew Nancy very well, but what I knew of her I liked."

I nodded. "Thanks—thanks for everything." Then I kissed her, for the very first time.

Then we said good night, and I turned out the living room lights and moved my books into the bedroom to study.

The pattern of the following week, already outlined, was filled in in detail on Monday.

Gary woke up a little after I did, and almost immediately found himself a bottle.

"Are you going to class?" I asked.

"Uh-uh."

"Do you think you'll make it to the office this afternoon?"

"I . . . I don't think so."

"Well, that's okay. Don't worry about it."

"Thanks."

"It's okay. You know where the food is, if you get hungry. And take another vitamin pill, huh?"

"Will do."

"Good. See you later."

"So long."

And I went to my morning classes, had a snack-bar lunch, and went to my afternoon classes. Then I went to the office. I felt like apologizing to Patty.

"About last night . . ."

"That's all right, Duncan. Really."

So we were pals again and I was a bit more comfortable. I was very businesslike for the rest of the afternoon. Then Patty gave me supper again, cooking and serving it in her own efficiency room. It was good. Meat loaf, which I didn't usually like—but this time very good.

When I got back to the suite, Gary passed out again. There was an empty Campbell's soup can on the kitchen table, along with some bread crumbs, so I knew he'd **at** least had something to eat. I spent the rest of the evening studying in my bedroom, then turned in early.

And that was very much the pattern of the week, with Gary drinking whenever he was awake, and Patty giving me supper. The only change was on Wednesday, with club dinner and meeting, and I had to explain Gary's non-appearance there.

Friday afternoon at the office Patty and I weren't getting much work done.

"Don't you think it's about time to get him on his feet now?"

"Yeah, I think so," I said. "I hope it isn't too late already."

"I only asked because it's getting so close to finals."

"I know. I've been in touch with his profs. They're all very sympathetic—but I can't expect their sympathy to go on forever. I've got a list of assignments they've given me for him—it's as long as your arm."

She nodded.

"I think we're going to have to put him on the wagon very soon."

After supper, Patty came to the suite with me to find Gary out as usual. I gave her the remains of my somewhat depleted liquor stock, along with the few beers remaining in the refrigerator.

"Shall I clear out his room too?"

"Would you? You still have the key, don't you?"

"Uh-huh."

"I'd appreciate it."

"He can go right out and buy more, you know."

"I know, but first I'm going to make sure he's sober and that he knows it's up to him."

She nodded.

"It's about all I can do."

"I know." She left with the bottles and cans and the assignment sheet to leave in Gary's room—and a little later brought Gary's key back. "He'll be needing this, I should think."

"I should hope so. It's not doing him much real good any more, playing permanent house guest."

"Good luck with the plan."

"Thanks. I'll need plenty." I closed the door after her and realized there was just one trouble—I wanted a drink. After making sure once more that Gary was secure in his unconsciousness, I left for one of the bars.

The next morning I woke well before Gary, if only because of my loud alarm clock. I had a bit of a head on and was determined not to let it show. I went rapidly through my showering, shaving, and dressing, and brewed up a big pot of strong coffee. I had some of it as I waited for him to wake up, and had to open a fresh pack of cigarettes to accompany it properly. This turned out to be the next to last pack in a carton I'd bought only Wednesday afternoon.

Gary finally woke up and automatically began prowling around for something to drink. "What happened to all the hooch?"

"I gave a big party last night. You missed the whole thing. Have some coffee."

"Ugh."

"Don't 'ugh' me. Have some coffee. It's good for you."

"Are you trying to tell me something?"

"You're damn right I am."

"Great. Now we've got Message. Let me get a couple of aspirin first."

I waved him off toward the bathroom and could hear him fiddling with the medicine cabinet and the water.

215

He came back and sat down at the kitchen table. "Now, then."

"Now, then, it's just that it's not much more than a week to go till finals, and it's about time you recognized the fact."

"Oh, hell, Duncan, I don't care. Give me a beer."

"There isn't one in the place. And whether you care about it or not, I'm not going to help you shoot yourself."

"Oh, Lord . . ."

"I'm going to sit here and watch you drink coffee until I'm sure you're absolutely sober. And I'm not going to turn you loose until you are."

He sighed. "Duncan, don't you see I just can't face it all again?"

"You're making excuses. You just want to curl right up —probably out of pure laziness."

"That's isn't true and you know it."

"Okay. But I know better than anyone else what you've been through—I was in love with her once myself."

"That was a long time ago."

"It wasn't such a long time ago. Things like that don't fit onto calendars very well. I know what you've been through, and I know that you've got to go back out now, if only with a view to taking revenge someday."

"That would be something. That'd be about the only thing."

"Okay. Drink your coffee."

We had three cups apiece, with many cigarettes.

"Oh, God," he said after a while, "my courses."

I couldn't help a short laugh. "It's about time you gave them some thought. I've been in touch with your profs all week, and they understand. There's a list of assignments waiting for you on your desk. You're going to have to work, but you aren't lost."

"Thanks. I guess I'm really going to have to dig in."

216

I nodded.

"Okay, I'll try. And thanks, Duncan. Even for that time at Connie's."

"That's okay. Just do one thing, huh?"

"What?"

"Take a shower sometime soon."

He called me that night, close to midnight.

"I wanted you to know I've been studying all day. I really think I'm going to be all right now. Thanks."

"Hell, I should be thanking you for giving me something to worry about and keeping *me* from going off the deep end too. I'm glad you're on your feet now. Let's just call it square."

"Okay."

"How's the work going?"

"Pretty well. I think I've got a chance of catching up, probably just in time for finals."

"That's certainly better than not at all. Oh, one other thing. If you have any trouble sleeping, let me know. I've got more of those pills around."

"Thanks. I hope I won't have to."

"So do I. Well, I think it's about time for me to turn in."

"Yeah, I think I'll be working a little longer myself."

"Don't push yourself too hard. You haven't got that little time, you know."

"I know. I should be okay. And Duncan—I'm not going to forget your suggestion—about revenge."

"Okay, so long as you don't just mean Connie."

"I don't. I didn't know what I was doing then."

"I'm glad you recognize that. By the way, if you do feel really pressed for time, Patty and I can cover for you at the office."

24

It was the last night of winter term. Finals had ended late that afternoon. I'd had one in the last slot and, rather than have to rush, I was leaving in the morning. Tonight I was packing, slowly and judiciously, and trying to unwind without the aid of alcohol. Then I answered the unexpected knock on my door.

"Gary. Haven't heard anything from you for a few days."

"I was digging in. I'd hoped you'd still be here."

"Yeah, avoid the rush and so forth. I can trust you with a beer now, can't I?"

"I think so. After these long, dry two weeks, I could use one."

"Fine." I got two cans from the restocked refrigerator. We sat down with them in the living room. "Did you have a late final too?"

"Yeah. I could have made the last bus, but I didn't want to. I'm going to stay up here over break."

"Why, for heaven's sake?"

"Research. How'd you do on exams?"

"Hell, I don't know. All right, I guess. I'll find out soon enough. You?"

"Pretty well, I think." He paused to light up a cigarette.

"I got up on everything in time, and in any case, I think the profs are willing to give me a break."

"Good. You look a little tired, but not too bad. What's this 'research' you mentioned?"

"Basically, it's just an extension of freshman orientation. I want to get to know the place a bit better."

"Looking for the secret passages?"

"Well, yeah."

"Great. I don't think there are any, but good luck. Really, why don't you want to go home?"

"Hell, Duncan, what could there possibly be there for me?"

I spread my hands. "That's one I can't answer. But do you really expect to accomplish anything by staying here?"

He spread his hands. "Can't know till I try it."

I nodded. "Sounds like something's in the wind, but I won't ask."

"Well, frankly, there's something I want to ask you about. Duncan, I'm going to try to find the underground. There's got to be one here, I know. You've been around a lot longer than I have. And if I can't ask you, there's no one I can ask. Do you know anything about it?"

I could only shake my head.

"Nothing?"

"Nothing."

"But I thought you'd know—I thought you might be one of the leaders. There has to be someone organized to fight back."

"No, as far as I know, there isn't. You know by now that the *Tumbrel* isn't a front for anything else. And there isn't any inner circle in the club—I know all the older members well enough to be pretty damn sure."

"Something else?"

"I really don't think so. Granted the *Tumbrel* and the

club are as far as my direct knowledge goes. But I think if there were something else, I'd know about it by now."

He grunted. "I didn't think it was going to be like this."

"I'm sorry."

"Me too." Then he chugged down the rest of his beer awfully fast. "Well, I'd better get going. I guess you've still got some packing to do."

"No, that's all right."

"I've got a couple of things I've got to see to yet myself." He stood up.

"Well, if you've got to go. One thing. Take it easy on the hooch, especially while you're by yourself."

"Don't worry about that. It's all over. I'm sure."

"See you in about a week and a half, then," I said.

"Right. Good night."

The bus I took out in the morning was practically empty and I'd missed the party-train by more than twelve hours. I sat by myself through the trip, smoking and occasionally reading in a thriller I'd bought at the railroad station. Into Grand Central finally, and then the creaky old Harlem Division out to Chappaqua—the trains that went out that far always had the crummy old cars.

That week or so back home was no better than usual. None of my old school crowd had break at the same time, not that they and I had much to say to one another any more.

It seemed I spent more of that week in the area bars than anywhere else. Most of the time I was by myself— just once I met a girl and bought her a few drinks, but then she didn't want to go anywhere with me and I resurrected my critical faculties to sour-grapes it for me—she had much too wide a mouth and thin legs. Most of the time I was by myself. No toasts, no songs. Now that Gary was in the clear, I came close enough to using his method myself.

I'd brought my little bottle of sleeping pills home with me and was careful to keep them out of my parents' sight. The pills helped very nicely to clear away the dreams I was having too often—always about Nancy.

The folks never did find out about the sleeping pills, thank God, but they did soon come to suspect me of about one-tenth the drinking I was actually doing, and were consequently very worried about me.

For their sake more than mine, I put a tighter rein on myself for the few days of break remaining. Soon enough I was on my way back to MU, cheerfully taking part in the fun of the party-train, but with a sense of expectancy underneath.

The first day back at school, Gary showed up at the office in uniform, with two black term-ribbons over his breast pocket.

"Congratulations," I said.

"Thanks. How'd you come out?"

"High mid-range. Good enough for me, for now. How was break?"

"Pretty good. I probably know the Tower and the campus as well as anyone else you'd care to name."

"Very good. Any secret passages?"

"No, but I did manage to get onto the unopened floors. Have you ever seen them?"

"Yes."

"You have? Quite something, aren't they?"

"Uh-huh. You were a little surprised to find that they're fully equipped?"

"Yeah, I was."

I nodded. "Just goes to show that when this place was set up, the people who were paying the bills were able to see that things were done the easy way."

"Easy when you've got the money."

"They've got it all right. By the way, I thought that those floors were supposed to be locked."

"They are, but I discovered that there are ways to get around locks."

"So did I."

"Uh-huh. The only place I couldn't get into was the power plant."

"Not surprising—you might see about going on one of the tours through it sometime, though."

"Good idea. Say, did you know that 'campus' originally meant 'battlefield'?"

"Does it seem relevant?"

"Kind of."

I nodded, then lit up a cigarette. "You're really going to try to find your underground, aren't you?"

He nodded.

"Well, you know I'm not overly optimistic about your prospects, but would you let me try to help you with it?"

"Duncan, I know I owe you a lot—an awful lot—but on this—no."

I leaned back in my chair, nodded once and took a puff from my cigarette. I felt very old.

At the office Gary worked efficiently and quietly, not as he had when he'd been mimicking me but simply as if he wished to spend as little time as possible on the job and as few extra words as possible on Patty and myself. She chalked it up to his continued reaction to Nancy's death, and I didn't then bother her with the specific details.

He had been writing up until Nancy's execution, working on his MU-picaresque. That, of course, was all over now. He wrote an ending, entirely out of keeping, which in two pages had his hero executed out of the blue. I argued with him about it but he insisted, and the rest was so good that I agreed to run it with his ending.

In a way I saw more of him at once-a-week club meetings than at the office every weekday. Here he made the effort to be affable, and did it well. I watched him become one of Tom Curtis's more intimate cohorts. I said nothing about him to Curtis, but Curtis seemed pleased to tell me that he'd just given my old protégé an appointive post in Student Government, a minor one, granted, with no real authority or responsibility but with an ear on every department.

I told Tom I was very pleased, and I was, if not in the way he thought.

My own living ways by now were back to the pattern of the past fall, only more so. I kept to my suite more than ever, going out for almost nothing but classes, work at the office, and club meetings. I never had guests in my suite. I had abandoned "Who Is Duncan Chase?", at least for the time being.

Patty tried to keep an eye on me, still invited me to dinner every so often. And then I'd return the favor by inviting her out to dinner. I didn't tell her how glad I was for those invitations.

25

Gary was engaged with his search for an underground by now.

So that he might be more useful to it once he had found it, he already had an excellent cover built up. His grades were still high-range, he was on the *Tumbrel* and in Student Government, and gave the impression on the whole of being a pleasant, hard-working, safe, locally-ambitious student.

He committed nothing to paper, but kept in his head a juggle of running evaluations of individuals and groups, constantly shifting but always working out to the same thing: nothing.

It didn't take him long to find out what he wanted to know about Student Government. It operated almost exactly as it said it did. It was responsible for a surprisingly large part of the actual running of the University—the details that pertained to the convenience and comfort of students—leaving the faculty as free as possible for teaching and research, and leaving the actual Administration as small as possible. There was a little graft, but apart from that, Student Government was just what it said it was.

The individuals in Student Government took somewhat longer to evaluate. The general plan was, on meeting a person who seemed could be a possible member of the underground, to strike up a rapid acquaintance, suggest a couple of drinks, and there, in a quiet bar, start a mild line of anti-Self-Discipline talk and see where it might lead. It never led where he wanted to go. There were malcontents enough, even in Student Government, but no one to offer to sign him on.

He would have resigned his little position except that he was sure it would be useful, once he'd found the underground, for blackmail or sabotage.

Once he felt he knew Student Government and was sure that it did not contain what he was after, he started trying the other groups. Even though he couldn't touch the other social clubs, there were still more than enough groups to try, most of them centered upon special interests of one kind or another.

Here his pattern was first to spend an afternoon in the library, researching the particular interest involved, then to go to an open meeting of the group, where he would make no pretense of being anything more than a novice in the field. With luck, the evening would end with beers with some of the members, preferably with officers. It was easy enough—many people remembered his name from the *Tumbrel*—but despite his affability and careful patter directed against the Self-Discipline Plan, he still got nowhere.

It was getting a bit discouraging.

He hadn't passed more than hello's in the hall with Keith Frazier since the past fall, but Gary remembered him as being extremely skeptical of the University Administration even then. Frazier was in Compass social club, along with Art Liebman, and that was one of the few groups that Gary could not feel out directly. He made a point of dropping in on Frazier one day.

"Hey, have a seat, Gary. Seems like ages since we've talked."

"Thanks."

There was a swapping of recent personal information, the usual talk about grades, activities, and how their two clubs were doing. After a while Gary was able to steer the conversation his own way. Frazier knew, if from a considerable distance, the story about Nancy, and consequently Gary was able to be completely open in his hatred for the Self-Discipline Plan.

Frazier felt the same way about it—to a point. "I know it's rough—God! I can imagine what you must have gone through. But you see, I'm trying to be careful, to look out for myself. That's what you've got to do. Right now I'm still running in high mid-range. Nobody chops my head off and nobody holds any grudges against me. And there's an awful lot you can still get from this university—and I don't just mean the social life. You know what the deal is on hiring from here—you've heard the stories about who some of the people are who endowed this place. You know they say in thirty years, MU grads will hold half the key positions in the country."

"I know," Gary said, and afterwards excused himself as rapidly as he could.

It got very bad. He was still dreaming about Nancy, and would not go to the infirmary for a prescription for dream-killing sedatives. His days were always purposeful but they were also always fruitless. There was a built-in fog to them after a while, as if he were always drunk, although he now drank only when socializing required it, and very little even then. And in some of his dreams about Nancy, he was the one who pulled the cord.

There was another dream he had once during this period, a quieter nightmare. It was the night after he had researched the game of Go and then attended a meeting of the MU Go Club. He had thought it inoffensively esoteric enough to perhaps provide an excellent front for operations. He had been wrong, of course—the MU Go Club proved entirely inoffensive, except on its own playing boards. He chided himself for not having realized that game-players would be this way.

In the dream that followed, he was in his room late at night, reading, when the president of the Go Club, a Rex Thiel, silently entered the room and motioned that Gary should follow him. They went wordlessly through hallways and down elevators, and Gary became lost, despite the training he'd given himself over break.

They came to a door, which Thiel opened for him. Inside was a room as large as the Main Auditorium, and at its center was a huge Go board. It wasn't a standard board scaled up, but a board with thousands of lines at just the normal spacing.

Someone filled Gary's hand with playing-stones. Some of them were white and some were black. Gary turned to ask Thiel how he should play them but Thiel was gone.

There were many people around the board, all playing stones. Gary recognized Frank Pryor, his floor supervisor, and Tom Curtis and many others from Student Government. His adviser, Dr. Loft, was there, as were all the instructors he had had. President Clark was there too.

"How do you know how to play your stones?" Gary asked the nearest person, who happened to be President Clark.

"You can't know. You just play them and hope for the best."

228

Gary made a play that completed the capture of a group of black stones, which immediately disappeared. "Have you tried putting a computer into the play?" Gary asked Clark.

"Of course, but the instant we plugged it in, the board doubled in size. It's still growing, all the time. If you watch closely, you can see it."

Gary watched, and out of nothing the board extended itself, adding another line each way. Then he managed to wake up.

He found no playing-stones still in his hand, and was thankful. He got up and went to the bathroom to clean himself up. He stared at his reflection in the mirror for a few moments but could get nothing from it. It was the message sent too often.

It went on for weeks. Finally at one of the club meetings I saw that he wasn't looking well at all, and spoke to him about it.

"What about it?"

"You aren't sick, are you?"

"No, I'm not sick."

"Look, Gary, I have a pretty good idea of what you're doing. I don't think you ought to push yourself so hard."

"Cut it out. You aren't my doctor, remember. You're the Administration's tame gadfly."

"Gary . . ."

"Look, you say you know what I'm doing. I don't think you'd turn me in. But even so, I don't want to have anything to do with a sellout."

26

Gary didn't show up at the office the day following our interchange at club meeting, or the next day. That night, Patty and I were sitting quietly in my suite when Gary called.

"I'm sorry about what I said the other night, Duncan." His speech was badly slurred. "I really am. Could you please come over?"

"Sure, be right there."

"Thanks."

"It's okay. See you soon." I put down the receiver.

"What's the matter?" Patty asked.

"It's Gary. I'll try to be back soon."

"Okay."

I kissed her once, quickly, then went to Gary's room. He was most definitely drunk.

"Duncan, I can't find it—there's no underground."

"I know. Take it easy."

He started being sick, as much from fatigue as from alcohol, by the look of him. Luckily, the run to the bathroom was shorter in his place than in mine and I got him to the bowl on time. Still he was trying to talk, between retches. "D'you understand, Duncan? There's no underground, no underground at all."

"I understand, Gary. We'll talk about it in the morning."

"But . . ."

"No buts. As soon as we get your system cleaned out you're going to bed and I'm going back to my paramour."

"But . . . Your paramour?"

"My paramour. Patty. As of last night. Okay?"

"Yeah, okay."

He was empty now, and fortunately wasn't dry-heaving. I got him to his couch and left.

It was close to eleven the next morning when he came by. He was dressed neatly, appeared to be sober, and looked as if he'd had a decent meal for a change.

"Come in," I said. "You're looking better now."

"Thanks. Hi, Patty. Congratulations."

"Thanks, Gary."

"You too, Duncan."

"Thanks. Would you like a cup of coffee?"

"Yeah, thanks."

Patty went and got two fresh cups, handed him one as I indicated the armchair to him, and gave the other to me. "Gary, would you excuse me? I've got to do some shopping."

"Sure."

"See you later." She grabbed her purse and left.

"Okay," I said after the door was shut, "do you still want to talk about it?"

"There's not that much to say. It's just that by now I'm absolutely convinced that there is no underground here."

"You're really sure."

"As sure an anyone can ever be of anything."

I nodded. "I didn't think there was one." I paused to

light a cigarette, that emptiest of actions. Gary got out one of his own and took a light from me.

"I wanted to tell you," he said, "because now I know I owe you an apology."

"I won't accept it, since I don't really know whether you owe me one or not."

"Accepted or not, it's there." He took a sip from his coffee. "And now I really need your help."

"With what?"

"With finding out what's next. Just where do I go from here? How do you survive at MU?"

I laughed, just a little. "Now you've really touched the unanswerable. Do you mean, how does one survive here in general or how do I myself survive specifically?"

"You yourself, for a start."

"Not too well, as you should have seen by now. No, really, Gary, even that is one hell of a question."

"Duncan, I'm sorry, but I've gotten to the point where I've got to ask the 'hell of' questions and try to get some answers."

"You're right. I'm sorry. Okay, Duncan Chase's MU Modes of Survival. I should be able to tell you something about them, I've been working on them long enough. Just don't expect me to be too clear. I've never tried formulating them before."

"Go on, please."

"Okay. To begin with, I'm afraid I'm a bit more phlegmatic than you are. But maybe that's not major. Satire is very important to me. I think it probably is to you too— the way I know you can write it. What I don't know is whether I'm using it as a drug or as something more. I hope it's something more. God*dam* it, Gary, you don't just sit down with a cup of coffee on a Saturday morning and ad lib a credo."

233

"I know, but please try."

"Okay, do you know what I mean about satire?"

"Yes."

"Good. Sometimes I think it's the most powerful tool available. Sometimes it seems like it's the only tool."

"But not all the time."

"No. There certainly ought to be other things. There *is* something else. I know. If you're in low-range and your number comes up, and you can walk down to the middle of the arena the way . . . the way Nancy did . . . then you've got it."

"I know." He spoke very softly and nodded. "I know."

"Right. There's something in a person that never has to surrender."

He nodded again.

"And quite frankly," I went on, "there's an awful lot in our little world that's quite acceptable. The Good Life isn't all hogwash—it makes for a partial balance, if only a partial one. And you can find things that are agreeable to you, and then you can hold to them for as long as they'll last. Some of them are very, very good."

"Like Patty?" He smiled.

I nodded minutely, also smiling. "Uh-huh . . . and re-member, I lost Nancy too."

"I know."

"You don't have to be hard-boiled about it, but you can get along, at least as well as the next guy. You'll never be completely free from troubles, but neither will he. The course of True Life ne'er runs smooth, etcetera. . . . Do you see what I'm driving at?"

"I do. Very definitely. I'll try, Duncan, I'll try."

Then the klaxons went off.

Very deliberately we set down our coffee cups and ground out our cigarettes. I locked the door after us— Patty had my spare key so there was no problem there—

and we started off down the hall. I glanced just once at Gary's face as we walked, and was relieved. I had never seen him look so calm.

The slowly-moving lines of students got thicker as we got closer to the Main Auditorium. Some were in bathrobes and slippers—hell of a way to meet your Maker, I was thinking.

Patty was in high middle-range like me, but I was still relieved to see her waiting for us at the nearest Auditorium entrance. I took her hand and she, Gary, and I went inside. We took the nearest free seats. Patty was squeezing my hand tightly and I maintained the return pressure. Gary was sitting with his hands in his lap.

The floor supervisors went into their huddle, then came out of it and closed the doors. The klaxons stopped and the administrator came forward.

There was no trouble with the microphone this time. "John B. Castle," the administrator said.

An ordinary-looking young man rose from his seat at the far side of the arena. He moved slowly at first, then gained speed as he got closer to the center. His face seemed completely expressionless.

I didn't know him, and nothing on Patty's or Gary's face indicated that either of them did.

"John B. Castle," the administrator said, "Your name has been selected at random from those of students whose grades have fallen below the minumum acceptable level. Do you understand?"

Castle nodded slowly.

"Gary J. Fort," the administrator said, and somehow it didn't surprise me.

I looked at Gary. He seemed startled, but only for an instant. I put my free hand on his shoulder, in an attempt to brace him.

A small smile started on his face. He shrugged my hand

off his shoulder and stood up. He began edging his way through the row and then walking down to the front. The damned fool was laughing.

I wanted to stop him. I wanted to jump up and throttle him. Instead I sat motionlessly in my seat, dreadfully afraid of what I knew he was discovering.